Giambatista Viko; or,
The Rape of African Discourse

GEORGES NGAL

Giambatista Viko; or, The Rape of African Discourse

Edited and Translated by
David Damrosch

The Modern Language Association of America
New York   2022

© 2022 by The Modern Language Association of America
85 Broad Street, Suite 500, New York, New York 10004-2434
www.mla.org

To order MLA publications, visit mla.org/books. For wholesale and
international orders, see mla.org/Bookstore-Orders.

The MLA office is located on the island known as Mannahatta
(Manhattan) in Lenapehoking, the homeland of the Lenape people.
The MLA pays respect to the original stewards of this land and to the
diverse and vibrant Native communities that continue to thrive in
New York City.

Cover illustration: *Faces VI*, by Angu Walters, ArtCameroon.com.

Originally published in France under the title *Giambatista Viko
ou le viol du discours africain*. © 3ème edition L'Harmattan, 2003,
www.harmattan.fr.

Translation © 2022 The Modern Language Association of America

Texts and Translations 39
ISSN 1079-2538

Library of Congress Cataloging-in-Publication Data

Names: Ngal, M. a M. (Mbwil a Mpaang), 1933- author. | Damrosch,
    David, editor, translator.
Title: Giambatista Viko : or, The rape of African discourse / Georges
    Ngal ; edited and translated by David Damrosch. Other titles:
    Giambatista Viko. English | Rape of African discourse
Description: New York : The Modern Language Association of America,
    2022.
Series: Texts and translations, 1079-2538 ; 39 | Includes bibliographical
    references.
Identifiers: LCCN 2021050604 (print) | LCCN 2021050605 (ebook) |
    ISBN 9781603295840 (paperback) | ISBN 9781603295857 (EPUB)
Subjects: LCGFT: Novels. Classification: LCC PQ3989.2.N462 G513
    2022 (print) | LCC PQ3989.2.N462 (ebook) | DDC 808.83—dc23/
    eng/20211202
LC record available at https://lccn.loc.gov/2021050604
LC ebook record available at https://lccn.loc.gov/2021050605

Contents

INTRODUCTION

Published in 1975 on the cusp of our global era, *Giambatista Viko; or The Rape of African Discourse* is an exceptionally timely work today—and a delight to read. Georges Ngal's self-obsessed antihero is an African intellectual eager to make a name for himself on the world stage. Professor at an unnamed university, Viko belongs to an institute of African studies that is riven between Europe-centered cosmopolitans and xenophobic Africanists who reject Western culture out of hand. He has been struggling for two years to write the great African novel, a work that he longs to finish so that he can be invited to conferences in Paris and Rome. Yet instead of writing he spends his time on the phone with his disciple and sidekick, Niaiseux ("Simpleton"), scheming against his Africanist colleagues, developing a cutting-edge theory of writing, and looking for ways to pad his résumé.

Viko knows that he has to produce a major work if he is to achieve his goal of becoming "le Napoléon des lettres africaines" ("the Napoleon of African letters"),[1] but he is aware that blending African and European cultures is no simple matter, even as he believes that Africa can no longer be held apart from Europe. For all his vanity and self-promotion, Viko is a shrewd observer of the scene around him; he sees "africanolâtrie" ("Africanolatry"), for example, as a subtler form of westernization. Casting about for inspiration, he recalls the *Scienza nuova* (*New Science*) of his namesake, the

Italian humanist Giambattista Vico, whose 1725 treatise asserts that all language began in the poetic cries of primitive people. Inspired, Viko decides that he can plunder African oral traditions to create the revolutionary novel that will be his ticket to international fame. (Appropriately, although "Giambattista Vico" and "Giambatista Viko" are spelled differently, they sound almost the same when spoken.) Viko reaches the point of writing, using an extravagantly experimental style: "tantôt des brusques opacités, tantôt des profondes transparences. . . . La ponctuation? N'en dis rien" ("abrupt opacities here, profound transparencies there. . . . Punctuation? Don't even mention it!"). His goal is within his grasp; but then disaster strikes. The Africanists gain the upper hand at his institute, and they go public with a series of accusations against him: of having his articles ghostwritten; of outright plagiarism; of sexual indiscretions with an Italian associate, a devotee of free love and French erotica; and above all, of betraying Africa by plotting to prostitute the mysteries of oral culture for Western exploitation—in the novel's subtitle in French, *viol* can mean either rape or a legal violation, and the term also suggests the theft, *vol*, of African discourse. Outraged, a group of tribal leaders arrest Viko and Niaiseux and stage a show trial, which concludes with devastating—but ultimately rejuvenating—results for our hero and his friend.

An extraordinary satire of problems of identity in a globalizing world, *Giambatista Viko* is a pathbreaking exploration of the vexed relations between European metropolitan centers and peripheral former colonies. Ngal's own life has spanned the globe, with periods spent living and teaching in Africa, Europe, and North America. He was born in 1933 in what was then the Belgian Congo, and he came of age during the country's struggle for independence.

Bilingual in French and in one of the Bantu languages, he studied Latin and Greek in Jesuit schools and then in a seminary, where he joined the Jesuit order. In a 1975 interview, "Authenticité et littérature" ("Authenticity and Literature"; G. Ngal, *Œuvre* 2: 197–210), he said that his teachers "se caractérisent par esprit libéral et humaniste. Ce qui développait chez leurs élèves la contestation, l'esprit critique et anticonformiste. Chose extraordinaire sous le ciel colonial" ("were distinguished by a liberal and humanistic spirit. In their students this developed a contestatory, critical, and anti-conformist spirit; something extraordinary beneath the colonial sky"; 2: 197).[2]

Ngal went on to study philosophy and theology at Lovanium University in the capital, Kinshasa, graduating in 1960, the year that saw the establishment of the independent Democratic Republic of the Congo. He spent two years teaching Latin and Greek in a Jesuit secondary school, then went to Switzerland to pursue graduate studies in literature. After earning a doctorate at Fribourg in 1968, where he wrote his thesis on the Caribbean poet Aimé Césaire, he returned to his homeland as a professor of francophone literature at Lovanium University. He soon became the first Congolese to head the department, which was formerly run by expatriates from France. His life took an unexpected turn in 1971, when he fell in love. He left the Jesuit order and married, though he remained a lifelong Catholic, and his novels make frequent references to the Bible. He moved to the Faculty of Letters at the University of Lubumbashi, in the southeast of the country, where one of his colleagues was the novelist and critic Valentin-Yves Mudimbe. Mudimbe had also studied abroad, receiving a PhD in philosophy in Belgium before returning home to teach and write; he and Ngal developed a rivalrous friendship. Ngal then spent two years abroad, from 1973 to 1975, first as a visiting professor at Middlebury College and then under the auspices of a foundation that sent him to teach francophone literatures in two-week stints at a series of universities in Canada, Belgium, and France. He began with residencies at the Université de Québec and then at the Université de Sherbrooke in southern Quebec.

It was in Canada that Ngal determined to become a novelist as well as a scholar. As he wrote in "Impact migratoire sur l'écriture" (G. Ngal, *Œuvre* 1: 83–92), a late essay on the literary impact of migration, during his stay in Quebec City,

> Un après-midi, je descendis dans la vieille ville où une brocante avait lieu. Je tombai par hasard sur un vieux livre d'un auteur français. Le hasard voulut que j'ouvris la page suivante: "Pauvres écrivains africains!!! Quand ils se mettent à écrire, c'est toujours pour nous rabattre une seule idée: ce que leurs ancêtres leur ont légué à travers les mythes, les legends, les contes, etc." Ce reproche ne me quitta plus et s'installa en moi pour toujours.
>
> Quelques jours après, je me trouvai à Sherbrooke. Installé dans un hôtel, au premier étage. Toujours habité par l'idée reçue à la brocante de Québec. Je décidai sur le champ de répondre à cet écrivain. La premier phrase de ce qui deviendra *Giambatista Viko ou le viol du discours africain* fut écrite dans cette chambre. La rencontre ici fut dominée par un mot: écrire. Un petit mot tout bête, quelques lettres seulement, pour traduire un labyrinth de pensées ou de rêves, de mystères. . . . (1: 84)

I went into the old town, where there was a used bookstore. By chance, I came upon an old book by a French author. I happened to open to the following page: "Poor African writers!!! Whenever they set themselves to write, it's always just to fall back on a single theme: their ancestral heritage of myths, legends, tales," and so on. This reproach stayed with me and permanently installed itself in me.

A few days later, I was in Sherbrooke. Settled in a hotel, on the second floor. Still filled with the idea I'd received in the used bookstore in Quebec City, I decided on the spot to respond to that writer. The first sentence of what became *Giambatista Viko; or The Rape of African Discourse* came to me in that room. The encounter there was dominated by a single word: *write*. A simple little word, just a few letters, for translating a labyrinth of thoughts or dreams, of mysteries. . . .

He began working on his novel during the balance of his teaching tour, then completed it upon his return to Lubumbashi.

Once back at his university, he received a chilly reception from Mudimbe and other colleagues who regarded him as building his career abroad instead of attending to problems at home. As Ngal worked on his novel, the character of Viko took on various traits of Mudimbe, both in appearance and in his love of surrounding himself with disciples. Even so, Ngal probably expected his friend to be a sympathetic reader, as Mudimbe had published a well-regarded novel two years before, *Entre les eaux* (*Between Tides*), on comparable themes of cultural alienation. Mudimbe's hero, Pierre Landu, is a priest who has studied in Europe but then abandons the priesthood after his return to the Congo, where he enlists in a Marxist guerilla band. Landu never finds himself at home, however, as he is always caught between the shifting currents of cultures and of ideologies. Yet Mudimbe didn't appreciate Ngal's more satiric treatment of an alienated intellectual. Instead, he took the book personally, and he actually lodged a legal complaint against Ngal, accusing him of defamation. Remarkably, then, Ngal found himself— like his own protagonist—subject to legal action by his academic rival. This could be called a situation of life imitating art, though now Mudimbe was accusing Ngal's art of all-too-closely mirroring life. In an angry essay for a weekly newspaper, he claimed that Ngal's portrayal of Viko was a thinly disguised attack on himself and several colleagues, in terms that were "précises, publiques, méchantes" ("precise, public, and nasty"). He writes that "il ne s'agit pas de fiction pure mais d'interprétation mensongère des faits réels et d'attaques intentionelles, surnoises et malveillantes" ("this is not a matter of pure fiction but a deceptive interpretation of real events and intentional, sly, malevolent attacks"), and he concludes: "Il est dommage que le professeur NGAL ait besoin, pour créer une œuvre, de piller et de falsifier la vie ou les comportements de ses collègues" ("It is a shame that in order to create a literary work, Professor NGAL has needed to pillage and to falsify the lives or the behavior of his colleagues"; "L'affaire *Giambatista Viko*" [*Zaïre-Hebdomadaire*]).

The case was dismissed, but relations with his colleagues grew so tense that Ngal soon moved to a university back in Kinshasa. Even four decades later, in an essay collection published in Ngal's honor in 2014, the editor included an appendix that reprinted Mudimbe's attack ("L'affaire *Giambatista Viko*" [Cibalabala]) together with a defense of the novel in the same newspaper—which was unsigned but probably written by Ngal himself ("L'affaire 'Giambatista Viko'"). More than that, the appendix includes photocopies of letters proving that Ngal hadn't been expelled from the priesthood back in 1971, as his enemies had claimed, but had received permission from his bishop and from Rome to return to secular life in order to marry (Cibalabala 262–67). Old disputes die hard.

In the same year that he published his novel, Ngal also published, in Senegal, his illuminating study *Aimé Césaire, un homme à la recherche d'une patrie* (*Aimé Césaire, a Man in Search of a Homeland*). He went on to publish extensively on Congolese and other African writers, and he was appointed a professor of francophone literature at the Sorbonne in 1980. He taught there and elsewhere in Europe until 1991, when he returned to Kinshasa to serve on a national educational commission. He was later elected to the Congolese parliament, and worked for many years with UNESCO and other international organizations before eventually retiring to France.

Quite apart from individual rivalries, the conflictual academic situation in the seventies reflected the tumultuous politics of the country as a whole. Following decolonization in 1960, the leaders of the newly independent Democratic Republic of the Congo were divided between westernizers and nationalists who wished to emphasize African cultural identity. Such conflicts could be found in many former colonies, but the Congo's colonial history had been particularly fraught. In the mid-1870s, having failed to persuade his parliament to establish a formal colony in central Africa, King Leopold II of Belgium set up a private corporation, loosely modeled on the British East India Company, which had become a de facto colonial power in India a century before. He treated the Congo thereafter as his personal possession. In 1885 his Congo Free State achieved international recognition, aided by the promotional work of the journalist-explorer Henry Morton Stanley. Renowned for having located the supposedly lost explorer-missionary David Livingstone deep in the forests of Tanzania, Stanley went on to dramatize his African adventures in bestsellers such as *Through the Dark Continent* and *In Darkest Africa*. He served for a decade as King Leopold's principal agent in creating trading stations along the Congo River and establishing relations with tribal chieftains. He detailed his success as colonial empire builder in *The Congo and the Founding of Its Free State: A Story of Work and Exploration*, which is filled with praise of "the munificent and Royal Founder of the Association Internationale du Congo" (386).[3] In 1899, Joseph Conrad drew on Stanley's works, as well as his own experience as a steamboat captain on the Congo River, for his novel *Heart of Darkness*.

Growing international outrage at the violence and naked exploitation in the colony forced Belgium to assume formal control in 1908 with the establishment of the Belgian Congo, though foreign commercial interests continued to play a major role in the colony. What had been de facto slavery in the Congo Free State was gradually replaced by wage labor, and an increasing number of people moved into urban centers, where there developed a Europeanized middle class, whose members were known in the patronizing term of the day as *évolué* (evolved) Congolese. A growing number of them began to receive university educations abroad, or in the Congo itself after several universities were founded in the 1950s.

Economic development went along with simmering political conflict, and an increasingly radical independence movement achieved the Congo's independence from Belgium in 1960. The new Congolese government was formed through an uneasy alliance of leftists and liberals, with the Marxist prime minster Patrice Lumumba governing together with the pro-American Joseph Kasavubu, who served as president of the republic. This government rapidly fell apart, and a civil war ensued, fueled by separatist movements in two of the country's richest provinces. The involvement of private militias hired by Western mining companies made the situation worse, as did Cold War maneuvering by the United States and the Soviet Union, each of which sought to use the conflict to advance its own interests in the region.

Lumumba was assassinated by opponents supported by Belgium and the CIA, and several chaotic years ensued. Finally, in 1965, power was seized by the army's chief of staff, Joseph-Désiré Mobutu, who established a dictatorial regime. He held power for over thirty years, murdering many opponents and potential rivals, all the while enriching himself and his cronies on foreign aid and through the expropriation of domestic industry. Mobutu cultivated close relations with Charles de Gaulle, Richard Nixon, and Romania's dictator Nicolae Ceaușescu (and later with Valéry Giscard d'Estaing, Jimmy Carter, Ronald Reagan, and George H. W. Bush), while also playing on nationalist sentiments. He renamed his country Zaire and promoted *zaïrianisation*, requiring his citizens to abandon the European names they had often been given at birth and to adopt African names instead. He dropped his own name of Joseph-Désiré and took the name of a warrior great-uncle, becoming Mobutu Sese Seko Nkuku wa za Banga (All-Conquering Warrior, Who Goes from Triumph to Triumph). As a result of this policy, during the 1970s Ngal ceased to write using his baptismal name, Georges, and chose instead the symbolic name Mbwil a Mpang (Spiritual Leader from Mpang).

It was under this name that Ngal published *Giambatista Viko* and a sequel, *L'errance* (*The Wandering*), which largely takes the form of dialogues between Viko and Niaiseux.[4] Their conversations are interspersed with appearances by Pipi de la Mirandole, whose name wryly recalls the great Italian humanist Giovanni Pico della Mirandola, famous for

his *De hominis dignitate* (*Oration on the Dignity of Man*). Viko
and Niaiseux debate questions of identity and the role of the
intellectual in society, as they rediscover the riches of African village life and as Viko works toward a fuller integration
of his European and African selves—the possibility of which
is still very much an open question in *Giambatista Viko*. As a
now wiser Niaiseux says at the conclusion of the sequel, they
have achieved a multidimensional and polymorphous mode
of communication. "Nous parlons en effet plusieurs langues,
témoins, dans ses paroles originelles, ses mots, ses tournures
de phrases, ces eaux profondes et différentielles qui constitu-
ent la diversité de l'humanité dans ses divers visages" ("We
really speak multiple languages—witnesses, in their original
modes of speech, their words, their turns of phrase, to those
deep and differential streams that constitute the diversity
of humanity in its many faces"; M. Ngal, *L'errance* 141). This
linguistic diversity goes along with a diversity of genre. In
both books, as Ngal later wrote in "Impact migratoire sur
l'écriture," he had no interest in writing plot-driven realistic novels: "C'eut été s'enfermer dans la suprématie d'un
genre; s'enfermer alors dans la tradition française et occi-
dentale" ("That would have been to enclose myself within
the supremacy of a genre, and so to enclose myself within
the French and Western tradition"; G. Ngal, *Œuvre* 1: 85).
His novels blend very different modes, including dream visions, essayistic discussions, extended quotations, and poetic
reveries.

By the time Ngal wrote *Giambatista Viko*, Mobutu's re-
pressive kleptocracy was in full flower, and open dissent
was impossible. Yet Ngal and other like-minded writers
fiercely maintained their independence. As Ngal wrote in a
retrospective survey, "Littérature zaïroise, cette méconnue"
("The Underestimated Literature of Zaire"; G. Ngal, *Œuvre*

1: 31–39), the literature of the period "n'a rien avoir avec la politique culturelle bidon du jour. Chacque auteur suit son inspiration, en toute indépendance. C'est là peut-être le plus significatif de la littérature zaïroise. Elle ne sacrifie ni au goût ni à l'idéologie du jour" ("had nothing to do with the drumbeat of the reigning cultural politics. Each writer followed his own inspiration, in complete independence. That is perhaps the most significant thing about Zairean literature: it made no sacrifices either to public taste or to the ideology of the day"). At the same time, "S'il faut lui chercher un dénominateur commun, il convient de reconnaître que c'est d'abord une littérature d'exilés de l'intérieur et de l'extérieur. . . . Un exil vécu comme une prise de conscience d'un déchirement culturel, d'une exclusion ou d'une séparation spatiale" ("If one seeks a common denominator in this literature, it is first and foremost a literature of internal or external exiles. . . . An exile lived as an awareness of cultural rupture, of an exclusion or of a spatial separation"; 1: 35). Mudimbe's *Entre les eaux* is one of the works that Ngal cites together with his own novel as examples of the literature of internal exile.

Giambatista Viko says nothing about national politics, but the show trial it depicts, and the tribal elders' brutal methods of punishment, clearly echo the regime's practices. Yet Ngal's trenchant satire extends to his own protagonist, hilariously dissecting Viko's vanity, self-promotion, and unstable mixture of insecurity and megalomania. In the novel's opening pages, Viko fawns over a visiting European intellectual, Sirbu, whose Romanian name casts an ironic glance at Mobutu's friendship with Ceaușescu.[5] Throughout the book, Viko compares himself to a pantheon of great French writers, while at the same time he obsesses over critical comments on the poverty of African culture by Jean-François Revel, who may be the unnamed writer whose condescending account of poor African writers had inspired Ngal to begin his novel in Quebec. Most notably, in his 1970 bestseller *Ni Marx ni Jésus* (*Without Marx or Jesus*), Revel had argued that revolutionary social change could be expected only from the United States and not from a stagnant Europe or an underdeveloped Third World. It would have been no comfort to the Francophile Viko that Revel had no more hope for progress from France than from Africa.

Ironically as he is presented, Viko is a surprisingly sympathetic character, embodying real tensions experienced by people with a foot in two different cultures. This situation has been acutely felt by many Congolese writers, participants at once in a multilayered African culture and a global francophone intellectual life; the Congo is, in fact, the largest French-speaking country in the world apart from France. If Viko bears a certain resemblance to Mudimbe, he is equally a portrait of his own author. Conversely, a description Mudimbe gave in an interview of his hero Landu could apply both to himself and to Ngal: "Il est africain, et viscéralement africain. Mais en même temps, il est occidentalisé, qu'il le veuille ou non. Ce qui fait de lui ce qu'il est, comme intellectuel, réside, justement, dans la complémentarité de ce double caractère: d'être, à la fois, africain et occidentalisé" ("He is African, and viscerally African. Yet at the same time, he is Westernized, whether he wants to be or not. What has made him what he is, as an intellectual, consists precisely of the complementarity of this double character: to be at one and the same time African and Westernized"; qtd. in Semujanca 23).

Giambatista Viko can be read at once as a Congolese novel, a francophone novel, and a contribution to world literature. Ngal had an encyclopedic knowledge of African literature both in French and in English, and his novel reflects his search for an alternative to what he saw as the dominant modes of folklorism and social realism in much of African fiction. In the broader context of francophone *littérature-monde* (world literature), he has Viko quote North African intellectuals such as the Algerian poet Rachid Boudjedra, as well as the *Cahier d'un retour au pays natal* (*Notebook of a Return to the Native Land*), by Ngal's favorite Caribbean author and longtime friend Césaire. In the background are Léopold Sédar Senghor's poetry and Chinua Achebe's 1958 *Things Fall Apart*, as well as Cheikh Hamidou Kane's *L'aventure ambiguë* (*The Ambiguous Adventure*), Ousmane Sembène's *Xala*, and other novels of the 1960s and early 1970s. Yet Viko, who looks down on his fellow Black Africans, never quotes them, and he doesn't realize that he is a far less exceptional figure than he supposes.

Giambatista Viko was part of a wave of African novels of the 1960s and 1970s written out of disenchantment with the results of decolonization. Where earlier works such as *Things Fall Apart* had probed the evils of colonialism, usually in a realistic mode, a range of African writers began to critique the authoritarianism and corruption of many postcolonial African regimes: for instance, Ahmadou Kourouma in *Les soleils des indépendances* (*The Suns of Independence*), written in exile from his native Côte d'Ivoire, and Sony Labou Tansi in *La vie et demie* (*Life and a Half*), written in a mode of magical realism, in which a dictator's victim refuses to accept his death and keeps reappearing in the story. Another notable example is Mali's Yambo Ouologuem, whose prizewinning historical novel *Le devoir de la violence* (*The Duty of Violence*) sharply critiqued the long involvement of Mali's rulers in the slave trade. Ouologuem's novel has further relevance because its author, like Viko, was accused of plagiarism; some passages of *Le devoir de la violence* were taken from novels by Graham

Greene and by the French writer André Schwarz-Bart. Stung by the controversy, Ouologuem retreated from writing, after publishing two further books the next year: a set of essays on the politics of race and gender, *Lettre à la France nègre* (interestingly translated as *A Black Ghostwriter's Letter to France*), and an erotic novel, *Les mille et une bibles du sexe* (*The Thousand and One Bibles of Sex*)—perhaps providing an inspiration for Viko's Italian girlfriend and ghostwriter Castino Paqua, who treats the French erotic novel *Emmanuelle* as her bible of free love.[6]

Ngal extends to language Ouologuem's critique of political and sexual violence. His alternative title for *Giambatista Viko, Le viol du discours africain* (*The Rape of African Discourse*), builds on a common trope of the European violation or rape of colonized cultures. This theme is found, for instance, in Wole Soyinka's 1975 play *Death and the King's Horseman*, and more starkly in the play's precursor, Duro Ladipo's *Oba Waja* (*The King Is Dead*), whose powerless hero Elesin declares that "My charms were rendered impotent / by the European" (81). As Maëline Le Lay has observed, in the 1960s and 1970s a number of African writers were seeking to reverse the European conquest; she quotes the Algerian writer Kateb Yacine's statement that "la langue française appartient à celui qui la viole et non à celui qui la caresse" ("the French language belongs to the one who violates her and not the one who caresses her"; 85). At the end of *Giambatista Viko*, Niaiseux becomes a direct victim of the warring masculinities around him.

Seduced by French culture, Viko constantly measures himself against French models: not only classic writers such as Honoré de Balzac, Gustave Flaubert, and Marcel Proust, but also the surrealists, in whom Ngal became deeply interested while working on his study of Césaire. Viko quotes

André Breton and the poets Robert Desnos and Michel Leiris, and he cites examples of the surrealism-inspired ethnography that sought to rejuvenate French culture through the study of traditional native societies. Atop the bookcase in his study sits a bust of the decadent poet Isidore Ducasse, self-styled Comte de Lautréamont, whom the surrealists had adopted as a precursor; the presence of the bust is appropriate, in view of the accusations leveled against Viko, since Lautréamont asserted that poetry is based on plagiarism.[7]

Further, the novel draws extensively on contemporary Parisian thought. Viko is a disciple of the Marxist philosopher Louis Althusser, and Niaiseux cites the psychoanalytic theories of Jacques Lacan. Viko's search for a dazzling new mode of writing owes a good deal to the theories of *écriture* (writing) developed in Paris in works such as Roland Barthes's *Le degré zero de l'écriture* (*Writing Degree Zero*) and Jacques Derrida's *L'écriture et la différence* (*Writing and Difference*). Ngal's novel can be read more generally as an academic satire, in the vein of David Lodge's *Changing Places* and *Small World*, both of which similarly hinge on rivalries between self-promoting literary and cultural theorists. But unlike Lodge, Ngal is seriously engaged in the theoretical debates he stages in his novel, and his tale has affinities with a tradition of philosophical fictions dating back to eighteenth-century works such as Denis Diderot's *Jacques le fataliste et son maître* (*Jacques the Fatalist and His Master*) or, a century later, Oscar Wilde's dialogues "The Decay of Lying" (*Artist* 290–319) and "The Critic as Artist" (341–407). Behind all these works stand Plato's dramatized dialogues.

As we read *Giambatista Viko*, we're constantly challenged to find our way amid the book's shifting currents of dialogue, reflections, dream visions, and sometimes brutal action. The primary focus of Ngal's novel is the contradictory yet complementary interplay between African orality and literacy derived from European culture. Ironically, Viko obsesses about recovering a lost orality while talking constantly on the telephone, sometimes to two people at once, a receiver at each ear. He doesn't even understand the Bantu language of the elders who put him on trial, and their speeches have to be translated for him by young up-and-coming technocrats. When Viko is accused of choosing "l'univers du livre—l'espace scriptural" ("the universe of the book—the space of inscription") in order to carry out his "tentative de désacralisation de l'oralité" ("attempt to desacralize orality"), he wonders whether the elders are really thinking in these terms or whether the translator is showing off his sophistication by embroidering their harangues; the elders' speeches come to Viko, and to us, thoroughly imbued with the Western discourse they reject. We also have to consider how far Ngal's own book embodies Viko's ideal for a new kind of *écriture*, and whether his novel does create the synthesis of African and European cultures that Viko apparently can't achieve but that his nativist accusers may not be able to escape.

Giambatista Viko is a creative contribution to the language debates also seen in English in the dispute between Chinua Achebe and Ngũgĩ wa Thiong'o on the merits and disadvantages of writing in English versus an indigenous language. Viko's search for an orally infused French can be compared to Achebe's rejection in the 1960s of the literary viability of local languages (such as Ngũgĩ's Gikuyu) and assertion of the need to write in the colonizers' language:

> Let us give the devil his due: colonialism in Africa disrupted many things, but . . . on the whole it did bring together many peoples that had hitherto gone their several ways.

And it gave them a language with which to talk to one another. If it failed to give them a song, it at least gave them a tongue, for sighing. There are not many countries in Africa today where you could abolish the language of the erstwhile colonial powers and still retain the facility for mutual communication. Therefore those African writers who have chosen to write in English or French are not unpatriotic smart alecks with an eye on the main chance—outside their own countries. They are by-products of the same process that made the new nation-states of Africa. ("African Writer" 58)

Achebe asserts that "for me there is no other choice. I have been given this language and I intend to use it" (62), even as he emphasizes that African writers need to remake English and French for their own purposes. Less high-minded than Achebe, Viko does indeed have an eye on the main chance, and yet he also embodies his creator's fascination with indigenous oral styles and performative modes of storytelling (a theme further developed in *L'errance*, which includes tales that Ngal's wife had recorded in Congolese villages). For Ngal, oral tradition involves individual creativity as much as tribal collectivities. As he wrote in a 1977 essay in the American journal *New Literary History*, "Beneath stereotyped formulas jealously retained by the conservatism and conformism of each generation, there occurs a true labor of creativity that is not the work of an anonymous community or of associations due to pure chance but is rather the product of the active dynamism of the individual genius" (M. Ngal, "Literary Creation" 336). Ngal's hero seeks to make his way between independence and authoritarianism, conformism and creativity, French culture and proverbial lore.

 Giambatista Viko is also a work in dialogue with world literature. At the time he decided to write it, Ngal had been voraciously reading world literature in French translation and in English. Viko quotes Johann Wolfgang von Goethe and Robert Musil and cites his namesake Vico's *Scienza nuova* by its Italian title, and he prides himself on his ability to drop English and Latin phrases into his conversation along with his many French references. When Viko and Niaiseux are thrown into prison, Niaiseux cheerfully anticipates serving as Plato to Viko's Socrates, hoping to record for posterity the final thoughts of his condemned master. In "Impact migratoire sur l'écriture," Ngal recalls that as he was working on the novel he drew on his experiences in Switzerland, Germany, and England as well as in Canada and France. His travels had included three months in England, where "la langue de Shakespeare résonnait en moi avec des accents particuliers. Une phonologie étrange! Séjours non extérieurs à mon écriture!" ("the language of Shakespeare resonated within me with particular accents. A strange phonology! Travels not external to my writing!"; G. Ngal, *Œuvre* 1: 85).

Though Ngal's frames of reference were primarily African and Western, he was already well aware in 1975 of a broader global world. Viko hopes to achieve worldwide fame, and having his work appear in the right languages is an important part of his plans. As he tells Niaiseux,

> Aucun savant aujourd'hui ne peut se passer de la connaissance de plusieurs langues internationales. Connaître l'anglais—je ne parle pas du français, la chose va de soi—l'espagnol, le russe, c'est bien. Le japonais, c'est encore mieux; le chinois c'est encore dix fois mieux car l'avenir, la clé de l'avenir, appartient à l'Asie, plus particulièrement à la Chine. Les Occidentaux ont terriblement peur du péril jaun. Mais combien de temps peuvent-ils pétendre tenir le coup.

Ils savent lutter contre la fièvre jaune, la juguler. Mais contre
la péril jaune, ils ne peuvent rien.

Des traductions ! Ça allongera la liste de mes publications.

No *savant* today can get by without a knowledge of several
international languages. To know English—not to mention
French, that goes without saying—Spanish, Russian, that's
good. Japanese, that's even better; Chinese is ten times better, since the future, the key to the future, belongs to Asia,
especially to China. The Westerners are terribly afraid of
the Yellow Peril, but how long can they hope to hold out?
They know how to combat yellow fever, arrest its spread.
But they can't do a thing against the Yellow Peril.

Translations! That will pad the list of my publications.

Not that Viko knows Chinese or Japanese himself; he plans
to ask his visiting colleagues Sing-chiang Chu and Hitachi
Huyafusia-yama to translate some of his articles. He wants
to get the essays published with the translators' names suppressed, so as to give the impression that he has done his
own translations. Marxist that he is, Viko has a passing
qualm about the ethics of exploiting his colleagues' labor in
this way, but Niaiseux reassures him that "[d]éontologique-
ment parlant" ("[d]eontologically speaking"), it isn't intellectual dishonesty at all, but simple collegiality.

Ngal's double-edged satire extends to the racially
freighted discourse in which Viko participates even as he
resists it. In the passage just quoted, Viko mocks the Westerners who fear what they describe as the "Yellow Peril"
without understanding that China is rapidly becoming
the political and economic equal of the West, soon to be
its superior. That Viko's institute hosts Asian and Eastern

European scholars situates it within the broad outlines of the Non-Aligned Movement founded in Belgrade in 1961 as an alliance of postcolonial and peripheral countries against the Cold War hegemony of the United States and the Soviet Union. Yet even as he asserts the equality of African and Western cultures, Viko allows that "d'habitude, j'ai un mépris du Nègre" ("generally I look down on Blacks"), and he gives Niaiseux credit for being only three-quarters Black, calling him "un métis" ("a half-breed")—using the racist term apparently in a positive sense. As Clarisse Dehont has observed of Ngal's portrayal of Viko,

> le fait que les propos racistes sont proférés par un Noir amène dans un premier temps de l'humour dans le récit, puisque le racisme est poussé à l'extrême par un personnage lui-même victime de propos stéréotypés et racistes au sujet de sa couleur de peau. Pourtant, l'objectif poursuivi, comme dans toute satire, n'est pas tant de faire rire le lecteur que de pousser celui-ci à une réflexion sur l'intériorisation par les Africains des stéréotypes les concernant. (166–67)

> the fact that racist remarks are made by a Black initially adds humor to the story, since racism is taken to the extreme by a character who himself is a victim of stereotyping and racist remarks concerning the color of his skin. Yet as in all satire, the objective is less to make readers laugh than to prompt them to reflect on Africans' interiorization of stereotypes about them.

Ngal's eminently worldly novel is a compelling meditation on the perils of identity and artistic creation in a world of unequal power relations, where vanity, self-defensiveness, and a will to power pervade every group. As such, *Giambatista Viko* gave no comfort to any side in the debates on decolonization and postcolonialism of the seventies and eighties, and it poses a continuing challenge to the optimistic notion that ideas and identities readily flow across cultures in today's global village. To date, it has received little attention beyond studies of Congolese literature, but with the Modern Language Association's two-volume edition, in French and in English, and with a Chinese version to be published as well, Ngal's self-promoting, self-reflective hero is finally achieving the global presence he always felt his genius deserved. *Giambatista Viko* is a novel whose time has come.

Notes

1. French quotations of George Ngal's *Giambatista Viko* are from the companion to this volume, published by the Modern Language Association of America in 2022.

2. Translations are mine unless otherwise indicated.

3. This phrase appears in a chapter focused on the difficulties of dealing with native middlemen in the ivory trade that was central to the economic exploitation of the Belgian colony. Stanley's chief conflicts are with a chieftain named Ngalyama, a landless slaveowner who "had nothing but his unfounded pretentions, his unreal claims, his loud bully's voice, and his insatiable appetite for the dues of blackmail" (Stanley, *Congo* 387). Ngal could have taken some of Viko's traits from Stanley's portrayal of the aptly named Ngalyama.

4. *Giambatista Viko* was first published by Éditions Alpha-Omega, in Lubumbashi, Democractic Republic of the Congo, and has since been reprinted by two French publishers, Hatier and L'Harmattan.

5. The philosopher and novelist Ion D. Sîrbu was imprisoned as a dissident from 1957 to 1963 by the Ceauşescu regime, a fact that may add to the suspicion surrounding Viko's dealings with foreigners. Sîrbu was little known internationally, unlike A-list figures such as Jean-Paul Sartre; Viko takes whoever he can get.

6. The translations of Ouologuem's three novels can be found in *The Yambo Ouologuem Reader*.

7. On Césaire's surrealism, see Michel 59–94. On the surrealists' championing of Lautréamont, see Ungureanu 88–111. Accusations of plagiarism have periodically been leveled against minority or non-Western writers who have appropriated elements from canonical works; see Miller.

Works Cited

Achebe, Chinua. "The African Writer and the English Language." *Morning Yet on Creation Day: Essays*, Anchor Press, 1975, pp. 55–62.

———. *Things Fall Apart*. 1958. Anchor Press, 1994.

"L'affaire 'Giambatista Viko.'" Cibalabala, p. 260.

Arsan, Emmanuelle. *Emmanuelle*. Éditions Fixot, 1988.

Barthes, Roland. *Le degré zero de l'écriture*. Éditions du Seuil, 1970.

———. *Writing Degree Zero*. Translated by Annette Lavers, Hill and Wang, 2012.

Césaire, Aimé. *Cahier d'un retour au pays natal*. L'Harmattan, 2012.

———. *Notebook of a Return to the Native Land*. Translated by Clayton Eshleman and Annette Smith, Wesleyan UP, 2001.

Cibalabala, Mutshipayi K., editor. *Le drame d'un intellectuel tiraillé entre discours occidental et discours africain: Mélanges offerts au Professeur Georges Ngal à l'occasion de son quatre-vingtième anniversaire*. L'Harmattan, 2014.

Conrad, Joseph. *Heart of Darkness*. Norton Critical Edition, W. W. Norton, 2016.

Dehont, Clarisse. *Des surhommes et des hommes: Regards croisés des stéréotypes à propos de l'Afrique et de l'Africain, de la littérature belge à la littérature congolaise*. 2012. U Laval, Quebec, PhD dissertation.

Derrida, Jacques. *L'écriture et la différence*. Points, 2014.

———. *Writing and Difference*. Translated by Alan Bass, U of Chicago P, 2017.

Diderot, Denis. *Jacques le fataliste et son maître*. Le Livre de Poche, 2019.

———. *Jacques the Fatalist and His Master*. Translated by Michael Henry, Penguin Books, 1986.

Kane, Cheikh Hamidou. *Ambiguous Adventure*. Translated by Katherine Woods, Heinemann, 1972.

————. *L'aventure ambiguë.* Julliard, 1962.

Kourouma, Ahmadou. *Les soleils des indépendances.* Éditions du Seuil, 1970.

————. *The Suns of Independence.* Translated by Adrian Adams, Africana, 1981.

Ladipo, Duro. *Oba Waja (The King Is Dead).* Translated by Ulli Beier. Soyinka, pp. 74–89.

Le Lay, Maëline. "Entre revolution et utopie: La littérature gestuelle de *Giambatista Viko; ou Le viol du discours africaine*: Une littérature populaire." *Aura d'une écriture: Hommage à Georges Ngal,* edited by Maurice Mpala-Lutebele Amuri, L'Harmattan, 2011, pp. 85–101.

Lodge, David. *Changing Places: A Tale of Two Campuses.* Penguin Books, 1979.

————. *Small World.* Penguin Books, 1995.

Michel, Jean-Claude. *The Black Surrealists.* Peter Lang, 2000.

Miller, Christopher L. *Impostors: Literary Hoaxes and Cultural Authenticity.* U of Chicago P, 2018.

Mirandola, Giovanni Pico della. *De hominis dignitate.* S. Berlusconi, 1994.

————. *Oration on the Dignity of Man.* Translated and edited by Francesco Borghese, Michael Papio, and Massimo Riva, Cambridge UP, 2016.

Mudimbe, Valentin-Yves. "L'affaire *Giambatista Viko*: La mise au point de Mudimbe." Cibalabala, p. 261.

————. "L'affaire *Giambatista Viko*: La mise au point de Mudimbe." *Zaïre-Hebdomadaire,* no. 376, 1975, p. 52.

————. *Between Tides.* Translated by Stephen Becker, Simon and Schuster, 1991.

————. *Entre les eaux: Un prêtre, la revolution.* Présence africaine, 1973.

Ngal, Georges (*see also* Ngal, Mbwil a Mpang). *Aimé Césaire, un homme à la recherche d'une patrie.* 1975. Rev. 2nd ed., Présence Africaine, 1994.

————. *Giambatista Viko; ou, Le viol du discours africain.* L'Harmattan, 2003.

————. *Giambatista Viko; ou, Le viol du discours africain.* Modern Language Association of America, 2021.

———. *Œuvre critique: Articles, communications, interviews, préfaces et études sur Commandes des organismes internationaux 1970–2009.* L'Harmattan, 2009. 2 vols.

Ngal, Mbwil a Mpang (*see also* Ngal, Georges). *L'errance.* 1979. Présence Africaine, 1999.

———. *Giambatista Viko; ou, Le viol du discours africain.* Alpha-Omega, 1975.

———. *Giambatista Viko; ou, Le viol du discours africain.* Hatier, 1984.

———. "Literary Creation in Oral Civilizations." Translated by Richard M. Berrong. *New Literary History,* vol. 8, no. 3, 1977, pp. 335–44.

Ouologuem, Yambo. *Le devoir de la violence.* Éditions du Seuil, 1968.

———. *Lettre à la France nègre.* Serpente à Plumes, 2003.

———. *Les mille et une bibles du sexe.* Vents d'Ailleurs, 2015.

———. *The Yambo Ouologuem Reader: The Duty of Violence, A Black Ghostwriter's Letter to France, and The Thousand and One Bibles of Sex.* Translated and edited by Christopher Wise, Africa World Press, 2008.

Revel, Jean-François. *Ni Marx ni Jésus: La nouvelle revolution mondiale est commencée aux États-Unis.* 1970. Rev. ed., J'ai Lu, 1973.

———. *Without Marx or Jesus: The New American Revolution Has Begun.* Doubleday, 1971.

Sembène, Ousmane. *Xala.* Translated by Clive Wake, Heinemann, 1976.

———. *Xala.* Présence Africaine, 1976.

Semujanca, Josias. "La mémoire transculturelle comme fondement du sujet africain chez Mudimbe et Ngal." *Tangence,* no. 75, 2004, pp. 15–39.

Soyinka, Wole. *Death and the King's Horseman. Death and the King's Horseman,* edited by Simon Gikandi, Norton Critical Edition, W. W. Norton, 1994, pp. 1–64.

Stanley, Henry Morton. *The Congo and the Founding of Its Free State: A Story of Work and Exploration.* Harper and Brothers, 1885.

———. *In Darkest Africa.* 1890. Charles Scribner's Sons, 1913.

———. *Through the Dark Continent.* 1878. Dover, 2011. 2 vols.

Tansi, Sony Labou. *Life and a Half: A Novel.* Translated by Alison Dundy, Indiana UP, 2011.

———. *La vie et demie.* Points, 1998.

Ungureanu, Delia. *From Paris to Tlön: Surrealism as World Literature.* Bloomsbury Academic, 2018.

Vico, Giambattista. *New Science.* Translated by David Marsh, Penguin Books, 1999.

———. *La scienza nuova. Biblioteca della letterature Italiana*, Pianetas-cuola / Einaudi, www.letteraturaitaliana.net/pdf/Volume_7/t204 .pdf.

Wilde, Oscar. *The Artist as Critic: Critical Writings of Oscar Wilde.* Edited by Richard Ellmann, Random House, 1969.

NOTE ON THE TRANSLATION

Georges Ngal's French is a pleasurable challenge to translate. As Samba Diop has put it, Ngal's style is "at once sober, polymorphous, undulating, and shimmering" (78). Viko's conversations and interior monologues unfold through eloquent meditations punctuated with sardonic interjections, and his double sense of himself as both an African and a French writer often plays out at the level of style. Much of the book's comedy stems from the contrast between colloquial, everyday conversation and the lofty Parisian academic-speak often used by Viko, Niaiseux, and even the tribal elders—or at least the young technocrats who translate for them. Fortunately, English has linguistic levels that are well suited to conveying this doubleness, since the Norman conquest brought an upper-class French overlay to England's indigenous West Saxon linguistic base. With its contrasts between concrete Anglo-Saxon roots and multisyllabic Latinate abstractions, English can effectively express Ngal's satiric style in a new idiom. In this respect the resources of English, grounded in medieval colonial conquest, may actually allow Ngal's postcolonial novel to gain in some ways in translation.

Latinate abstractions have so long been a part of English, however, that they no longer feel foreign to us. To suggest the exoticism of Viko's Parisian discourse, I have kept some of the French phrases Viko uses, in parallel to his periodic use of Latin tags. Such terms as *maître* (master), *le mot juste*, *le poète maudit* (the cursed poet), and *savant* (scholar) are thus more clearly marked as foreign in this translation than they are in Ngal's French text. For this purpose, I have retained French phrases that are fairly commonly used by somewhat pretentious English speakers, as a way to point up Viko's cultural double consciousness. Further, Viko shows off his sophistication by periodically using phrases in English; these are italicized in the original as foreign, and I have left them italicized in the translation to mark their foreignness. On the other hand, local Congolese terms that occasionally appear amid Viko's highly Parisian French, such as "mwambe," are footnoted but not italicized in the text, as they aren't foreign terms for Viko.

A particular question concerns the term *écriture*, which can generally be translated as "writing." Yet when Viko discusses his effort to create a revolutionary new style, his account has clear affinities with the theories of *écriture* being discussed in Paris during the 1960s and 1970s in the overlapping circles of poststructuralist theorists and practitioners of the *nouveau roman*. In such passages I have left *écriture* as an untranslated, italicized Parisian import.

A further question is how to translate the term *nègre*. Used in the eighteenth and nineteenth centuries as a general term for sub-Saharan Africans, *nègre* increasingly came to be used as a synonym for "slave," and even after the end of slavery it carried strongly negative connotations (Edwards 17–38). Starting in the 1930s, a group of writers studying in Paris, led by Aimé Césaire and Senegal's future president Léopold Sédar Senghor, sought to give a positive valance to the term. Césaire coined the term *négritude* to signify an affirmative connection to traditional African cultures and values, both in Africa itself and in the Caribbean. Ngal's hero is both a *soleil noir* (black sun) and an *écrivain nègre*, a term that would once have been translated as "Negro writer" but is the equivalent to "Black writer" in contemporary American English. Both *nègre* and *noir* can be used for the color or in contrast to *les blancs* (the Whites), of whose culture Viko both is and isn't a part. In the translation, "Black" is capitalized when either *nègre* or *noir* in the original French refers to a person.

This translation has benefited from a careful review by Bonaventure Muzigirwa Munganga, a Congolese comparatist now completing his PhD at the University of New South Wales, Sydney, who corrected a variety of infelicities and some outright errors in my draft and clarified Congolese cultural references and turns of phrase. I am most grateful for his patience with my prose and for his assistance in improving it.

Works Cited

Diop, Samba. "Georges Ngal l'essayiste: La racine orale et traditionaliste." *Aura d'une écriture: Hommage à Georges Ngal*, edited by Maurice Mpala-Lutebele Amuri, L'Harmattan, 2011, pp. 67–83.

Edwards, Brent Hayes. *The Practice of Diaspora: Literature, Translation, and the Rise of Black Internationalism*. Harvard UP, 1983.

GEORGES NGAL

Giambatista Viko; or,
The Rape of African Discourse

I

. . . Why this circle of hell imprisoning us? How to escape? By what witchcraft? If "impossible" isn't French,[1] "possible" isn't any more French than it is Black. Damn it! What saint is there to invoke?

"The airplane's just landed. You'll have to be the first one at the terminal. Every minute is worth its weight in gold; there's no time to lose. Friendship—when it's bestowed by a European—is priceless. I'm counting on our being the first to shake his hand."

She dashes off to the airport. Breaking the rule against nonofficial entry through the VIP lounge, she gets there first. The sky is radiant. Sirbu breaks out in a big smile, and with a wave of his hand he salutes the throng that's come to welcome him. She takes care to give her name: "Madame Giambatista!" She prolongs her handshake and conveys the greetings of her husband, kept away by professional obligations.

---

1. A favorite saying of Napoleon Bonaparte's to encourage his troops in the face of heavy odds.

"Merely a short delay, Madame—I already relish those hours of collaboration I shall spend with your distinguished husband, a black sun whom Africa is honored to count today among the most brilliant luminaries humanity has ever known!"

. . . Why this circle of hell, immuring us black writers? My novel is going nowhere even after two years, the ideas are bogged down, and meanwhile Revel's words keep coming back to me, obsessively: "They have no public. Their masses are illiterate. If they write, it is only to revive a bygone past that glows with the halo of the pompous label of a golden age."[2] Rousseauian anachronism. Affirmation of an always misrecognized identity. Anyone who tries to escape the trap rehearses worn-out phrases only good for feeding to moth-eaten Parisian pigeons. The more I chew over these ideas, accepted without debate, the more paralyzed I become.

I, who had sworn to be the African Chateaubriand,[3] I see the horizon closing in. All the same, the pen irresistibly attracts me. Then for whole days I don't manage

---

2. A quotation from the French journalist and philosopher Jean-François Revel.

3. In his 1802 work *La Génie du christianisme* (*The Spirit of Christianity*), the Romantic writer François-René de Chateaubriand included two novellas about noble savages in North America, inspired by his travels there.

to write a single line. I console myself with the thought that Flaubert took five years to write *Madame Bovary*. Why shouldn't I achieve as much myself? Even if it takes me ten years, fifteen? But it isn't the number of years' work that makes a writer. Orators are made but poets are born, as the saying goes—*nascuntur poetae, fiunt oratores!*

I seem to be excluded from the realm of letters. The thought of a critical acknowledgment of failure adds to my anguish an indefinable sensation of bitterness and impotence.

I've always believed that writing presents a singular response to existence. Always seen it as an instrument of liberation, the solution to my conflicts. Yet the gateway to the realm of liberation, of deliverance, seems completely shut. Curses on this paralyzing circle of hell! But suppose this circular logic were an ambush? The always "original," "culturally specific" form to judge Africans by? Giving up the pen, wouldn't that mean falling into the trap the Westerners have always set? . . . This new way to consider the echo of Revel's words cheers me up. Once again, writing seems to me to be a paradise of pleasures. The site where conflicts are resolved. Mirror of the reconciliation with ourselves and with others—a way out from ourselves toward others. A handle on alterity. Unfathomable locale where you lose yourself, like the *poète maudit*,[4] so as to find yourself again. What writer hasn't sought this negativity! Rimbaud, sacrifice offered up to all life's inebriations; Baudelaire, a human train wreck; Nerval, wide-open portal through whom all dreams flow. The African writer!...

"Giambatista, what are you doing? You look completely distracted! What are you daydreaming about?" my wife exclaims, shaking my arms.

"Oh! Yes . . . I was just thinking!. . ."

"Sirbu has arrived, all aglow. He knows you by reputation; he has expressed himself about you in exquisite words that have touched my heart. We'd better make the most of this first contact and win him over."

"It's up to us to initiate him. You know what has to be done. Not a minute to lose! We'll give a dinner for him tomorrow. You'll be sure to set out both my essays on the art of writing. Dazzle him! Nothing like a first impression. I'll see to it that this feast for the senses will also be one for the spirit. Among our faculty ranks, they all have so very little imagination that it's a real pleasure for me to orchestrate the conversation. The main thing is to come across as a brilliant conversationalist. Weigh

---

4. "Accursed poet," referring to a dissolute, antisocial writer, such as the poets Arthur Rimbaud (1854–91) and Charles Baudelaire (1821–67) and the visionary novelist Gérard de Nerval (1808–55).

my words well. A few well-placed flashes of wit . . . Sirbu will be all ours."

"Have you considered, darling, that tomorrow is the anniversary of the day you were awarded your doctorate? You might also invite our dear Niaiseux for this first meeting with Sirbu. That would help get him out of his solitude."

"Excellent idea! But I'm looking ahead too. He's the best example one could imagine for Sirbu—Niaiseux, who respectfully calls me *Maître*, is the guy who understands me to a T. Talking with him is a picnic. Perfect. Just think how he adores *le Maître*."

I think highly of him. He's just about my perfect reflection. Generally, I look down on Blacks. Though as for him, his blood is one-quarter foreign. A half-breed, like so many. But what I love about him is his almost feminine intuition of issues: the instinct that Bergson speaks about, that knows how to espouse different points of view; in short, my very being. That platter he presented me two years ago on my birthday, engraved with a shining sun—it's symbolic! A sun blazing through the shadows that cover the Institute. Despite his ridiculous name, through his friendship for me—well, I don't put much stock in friendship—through his identification with my system, Niaiseux is one of those people who can't live

7

without the image of someone they can identify with. If we have such success with the assorted foreigners who are among us, that's because they recover themselves in us. Ah, Europe, old Europe! She withdrew from our land too soon. But she isn't dead. With all their talk about Africanization, who among the Blacks at the Institute can hold a candle to Niaiseux?

"Hello, Niaiseux? It's *le Maître* calling! Could you join us tomorrow for an important dinner that we're giving for our new arrival, Monsieur Sirbu?"

"Certainly, *Maître*! Just two seconds before you called, I was coming toward the phone."

"Ah! A clear case of telepathy! For myself, I have a stubborn belief in it. Lots of phenomena can be explained that way. Love, friendship, clusters of common interests are telepathic states. I believe that Science will succeed in the not too distant future in formulating them mathematically."

"*Maître*, you have a gift for *le mot juste*.[5] I believe that all sorts of problems can be settled by telepathology, parapsychology, even by magic."

"Niaiseux, you're remarkable! You've spoken the words that have been on the tip of my tongue for the past

---

5. "The perfect word or phrase," which Gustave Flaubert always sought when writing his novel Madame Bovary (1856).

two years. I believe this is an experience that will put an end to my living nightmare of recalling something I read two years ago, just before I got to work on my novel. A man can't live on memories forever, at some point he has to look at what's going on around him. And as if by enchantment, you're putting me on the right path. Magic, daughter of witchcraft! That mode of speech that Firth recalls,[6] which is the discourse proper to primitive societies. A case that manifests social repression. Witchcraft—an ideological discourse! Region where hidden oppositions and latent contradictions are resolved. This discourse is what I need to tame. Whatever the cost!

"The lingering echo of Revel's words has made me into a kind of repressed man. Giving birth to any kind of literature has become painful for me. My fame as a black sun spreads around the planet, but my reputation as a writer is slow in building up. Only a discourse internal to Africa can liberate my own, enmeshed as it is in one of those sophisms that the Westerners alone can master. A subterranean life exists within us. Freudianism taught this to the West; but the primitives themselves have always been aware of it. From time immemorial, the interior life of individuals, as of society, has been ruled by

---

6. In *The Tongues of Men* (1937), the British linguist J. R. Firth explored the social roots of language in early societies.

this entreaty from below that Europe is only now beginning to rediscover."

"*Maître*, I've always said you were born too soon, a century ahead of our times. To tame our African discourse in order to liberate the West's paralyzed, repressed discourse—that seems truly inspired!"

"But consider! No ambiguity! I am of a race that cannot be assimilated to ordinary African writers. We have nothing in common but biology. My place should be in Paris, in Geneva. It's only an accident of history that had me born in Africa. To use a resource is not to assimilate. Picasso, Juan Gris, Lipchitz surrounded themselves with African masks solely to define their own aesthetic intentions; an Apollinaire trumpeted his desire to turn to fetishes from Guinea and Africa.[7] Let those misunderstand who wish. A means is a means. Don't lose sight of that.

"To give birth to a novel! In effect that means to take up a Western discourse. To develop a story within a visual space. In the spatial-temporal dimension. A yoke that strangely limits the writer's freedom: the possibilities of the discourse itself. The power of these dimin-

---

7. In Paris in the early 1900s, the Cubist artists Pablo Picasso, Juan Gris, and Jacques Lipchitz drew inspiration from African sculpture, as did the poet and art critic Guillaume Apollinaire, who coined the term *cubism*.

ished words loses the efficacy it enjoys in the magical universe of orality. A spoken word 'gives power over the thing named; the clay image represents the enemy you kill by piercing it with a needle.' It would take a *Scienza nuova* to rediscover the spiritual forces that our technological universe has lost and that have been preserved by the oral societies dismissively called primitive.[8] The power, the ability to decipher the language buried in the depths of symbolism: to decode the enemy's malevolent intentions. The secrets discovered constitute the great epiphanies of the divine beneath the veil of their surroundings—the viewer's essential domain."

"Your childhood was immersed in this universe!"

"Yet we've been torn away far too soon, plunged into the world of the written. We need to rediscover what we've lost. An acoustic space, or rather, an audiovisual one. That of the storyteller! What undefined riches! What freedom in the story's unfolding! None of the novel's rigidity! Novelistic space? A veritable circle of hell! I dream of a novel on the model of the folktale. Of a novel where the difference between the diachronic and the synchronic gets blurred—where elements of different ages coexist. Of a cinematic universe that creates an

---

8. Viko is here recalling the *Scienza nuova* (*New Science*) of the original Giambattista Vico.

order and is created by it; it's this fertilization of the novel by orality that I've been trying for two years to get myself to achieve.

"Can writing recuperate our destroyed childhood? A plausible hypothesis! One has to wager one's existence to survive. But that means to mimic these tales, these fictions, these tricks played by the gazelle on the leopard, tales that wove the fibers of our earliest childhood. To know where the discourse can create a flashback to take us back to what we've irremediably lost through a prematurely Benedictine education.[9] To be able to identify simultaneously with the discourse of the tortoise and the hare, of the maiden pursued by the ogress, to insinuate oneself into that of the lion, of the old woman with nine bellies, of the public under the moonlight, unmoved by rejection or exclusion, by approval or disapproval; to integrate the multiple lines of force ordering and breaking the frames, the procedures, controlling the storyteller's discourse; to use a whole bag of tricks to give a story its rhythm.

"Do you want to understand this *écriture* I dream of? It starts with the girl Nsole, born a cripple, on whom her father dotes to such an extent that he no longer wishes to

---

9. The Benedictine monastic order had sent many missionaries to the Belgian Congo, and the order's schools retained a considerable role after independence.

have any children but girls. One day, when her mother is soon to give birth, her father decides to go off to a distant village, invited for a gathering of his clan. Before leaving, he instructs his wife to keep the newborn if it's a girl, and otherwise to kill it. When the day arrives, the wife brings twin boys into the world. She hides them away, and when her husband returns, she presents them to him as serving boys. But one day, when they're away from home, Nsole betrays them. Enraged at having been deceived, the father decides to kill them, but when they're still far from home, they're mysteriously informed of what's being hatched against them. And so they get themselves to the house of the village chieftain's wife, who gives them two bottles to lodge in a corner of their house's roof. These will turn into prayer books that they carry everywhere with them. Yet one day the father grabs the younger of the twins and hands him over to the father's brothers as if he's wild game. Immersed in a barrel of boiling oil, he's saved by the older twin. At the same moment, their sister—who's been killed by the mother, whose secret she betrayed—awakens in the cemetery, and the father in turn takes his place in the pot. Magic. Bullfighting. Cannibalism. Marvels. Surprise. Treachery. The code of African art!"

"But the contemporary novel seems to have rediscovered the liberty you're seeking!"

"An illusion! Life is made up of illusions. It isn't enough to just destroy Balzacian space.[10] The contemporary writer hasn't yet reached the goal of his endeavor. He hasn't yet fully freed himself from the straitjackets of character and of the space-time continuum."

"In short, what you're insisting on is an absolute freedom?"

"Not necessarily. Nobody can escape from the space-time straitjacket. But to master it! That's the real problem."

"You think they've only taken their attempt halfway."

"Right! The novel's future lies in mastering this given. I'm working on it. To succeed in abolishing it—or more precisely, to create the illusion of having abolished it—that's the point on which I'm concentrating all my effort. I've almost gotten there. The poet Aimé Césaire, playing at being an African magician, timidly suggests this illusion:

> I remember the notorious plague that would break
>   out in the year 3000 there wasn't any star
>   announcing it just the earth in a wave
>   without pebbles kneading out of space

---

10. Referring to the realistic portrayal of ordered social life typified by Honoré de Balzac's panoramic series of novels, *La comédie humaine* (*The Human Comedy*, 1830–48).

a loaf made of herbs and confinement
strike peasant strike
on the first day the birds will die
on the second day the fish will wash up on shore
on the third day the animals will emerge from the
forest[11]

Just a simple grammatical exercise, perhaps? A *jeu d'esprit*? But the illusion created by magic was successful. The poet abolishes the classic distinction between the past, the present, and the future, installs himself in a kind of eternity. André Breton sought that 'point in the mind at which which life and death, the real and the imagined, past and future, the communicable and the incommunicable, high and low, cease to be perceived as contradictions.'[12] The French surrealist formulated the theory; it's up to us to illustrate it. In a way, the poets are ahead of us.

Circle of hell—space-time! The real problem is one of control and mastery. We aren't going to master it through rational rationality. A tale isn't what you think. It doesn't exist outside of the telling. At one and the

---

11. From Aimé Césaire's surrealistic poem "À l'Afrique" ("To Africa"; *Complete Poetry* 408). Translations of quotations in the novel are mine unless otherwise indicated.
12. Breton, *Second Manifesto* 123.

same time it's the surrounding scene, the actor, the public, the recitation. A novelist who could realize all these elements—what a performance!"

"Is such a literature possible? If it were, I'd call it 'gestural literature,' the same way one speaks of 'gestural art,' 'gestural painting.'"

"You've always wanted to go off the beaten track. This time, it seems to me that your research is heading straight for failure, for a gestural literature can't end up anywhere but the annihilation of the very idea of literature itself. Even if gestural painting—'art freed from constraints of technique, of predetermined images and of aesthetic considerations'—was possible, a gestural literature can never be achieved. I recall what Margit Rowell has written: 'The pictorial language of the West was elaborated according to the necessities of the representation of the object. To abolish the object in a radical fashion means abolishing certain conventions of design, color, composition that were invented as a function of the traditional relations of the artist to his object. . . . To abolish the object is once again to abolish the space the object occupies, and space is a determining element of painting. This means abolishing traditional components of spatial vision such as perspective, the picture plane, depth, proportions, extent, composition, organization, articulation, the relation of forms to a background or to other forms.'[13] We know that the champions of this new form of painting were obsessed by a quest for authenticity. But I believe that they sacrificed the aesthetic in the process."

"But what is the aesthetic—in an age when even ugliness has its beauties? Don't you know that what is called 'the fair sex' has useful lessons to give us? Every woman in the world, the 'ugly' like the 'plain,' has an admirer. The aesthetic is the daughter of education and of culture . . ."

My wife comes in. I hang up. Outside, the sun has made a *rendez-vous* with nature. Golden splendor. Beauty. Symphony of color. As if by instinct, the birds sense the radiant star's impending disappearance. The gris-gris utter screeches that are echoed by a chorus of squawking chickens and cooing doves.[14] All of nature seems to be complicit in its silence concerning me, my research. My newly recovered optimism doesn't give me mastery of *écriture*. Of space-time. Everything seems to have left me; my latent energies keep refusing to revive.

"Want to hear the latest? This is really rich!"

---

13. From *La peinture, le geste, l'action: L'existentialisme en peinture* (*Painting, Gesture, Action: Existentialism in Painting*; 10). In it, Rowell championed "la peinture gestuelle," which is concerned more with the act of painting than with the result.

14. Gris-gris are protective amulets that clatter together when worn around the waist.

"Sure—what's up?"

"A publication by X in the *Revue des sciences de l'homme!*"[15]

"That'll add to his CV! I've got to read it—but above all, I'll have to avoid mentioning it to the members of the Institute, make sure that the illusions that nourish that oddball don't take root more deeply from day to day. My indignation is visceral. There's only one person who can be talked about! Niaiseux understands. At the very instant I'm saying this to you, he senses it by telepathy. I don't want to act openly. Let's be subtle. I'll play a seductive role, then Niaiseux and all my devotees crowned with the pompous title of 'Associates' will carry it through . . . I'll just be the prompter. Like in the theater. Saving face. It'll cost him dearly, pretending to be an equal to *le Maître.* It won't take a lot. A sneering smile from the Associates when he passes by, repeated several times. A progressive isolation. The cancer of solitude will do the rest."

"Hello, Giambatista! Olobrinus here!"[16]

---

15. A reference to the *Revue des sciences humaines,* a leading French social science journal, in which Ngal himself had recently published an article, "Le théâtre d'Aimé Césaire: Une dramaturgie de la décolonisation."

16. The name Olobrinus likely evokes Olybrius, who was briefly installed as a puppet Roman emperor in 472 CE; in French tradition his name came to signify an empty-headed braggart.

"Yes, I recognize your deep, resonant voice."

"I've just heard about X's latest publication. This stinks. How could a journal of international reputation be so feckless as to publish a turkey like him? He can hardly even write the language. You'll have to make a reply in issue 10 to meet the challenge and shut this guy up once and for all!"

"I see it differently. The one foreigner who's on his side is rejoicing right now. The two of them are congratulating themselves on the allure that his renown, or let's say his, quote, unquote, 'scientific' reputation, is taking on. You know what has to be done. A conspiracy of silence. All our pals know the game. It's up to you to play it out. 'Why are all these usually friendly faces going blank? Even Olobrinus, he can barely bring himself to glance at me! Little groups are forming. When I pass by, sudden silence. Pursed lips. I hear whispers . . . Everything seems to be conspiring against me . . .'"

"Perfect. No better way to teach him a lesson. You have the gift of not just seeing reality differently but heightening it. Orchestrating things perfectly. Inspirer. Prompter. Actor. Spectator. All in all, you're the perfect illustration of your own research. A genius like you should be inducted into the Club of Rome."

"Just so. You always come up with le mot juste. I'm seriously thinking about it; my application is already drafted.

Since my research carries on in the direction of their report, the door should easily open wide for me.

Aurelio Peccei, Alexander King, Hugo Thiemann, Eduard Pestel, Saburō Ōkita, Adeoya Lambo, Adam Schaff—what a pantheon![17]

"Monsieur GIAMBATISTA, geniuses of your class have their place reserved in our Club. We are *au courant* with your research. A sun that daily pushes back the boundaries of the thick obscurity that covers the Dark Continent, that shines among us and bathes each of our members in an almost blinding radiance. Men of your caliber come along once in a century. Your contribution can help our studies take giant strides forward. One of our conclusions is as follows: 'We affirm finally that any deliberate attempt to reach a rational and enduring state of equilibrium by planned measures, rather than by chance or catastrophe, must ultimately be founded on a basic change of values and goals at individual, national, and world levels.'[18] It is appropriate for you, dis-

---

17. The Italian industrialist Aurelio Peccei and the Scottish scientist Alexander King founded the Club of Rome in 1968, bringing together politicians, economists, scientists, and business leaders from around the world to study global problems. Viko now imagines being inducted into the club and rehearses his acceptance speech.

18. From the Club of Rome's bestselling study *The Limits to Growth* (Meadows et al. 195).

tinguished Colleague, to bring about this transformation of values."

"Thank you, Monsieur le Président and dear Colleagues. The words of the eminent and distinguished *savant* Monsieur Aurelio Peccei leave me in some uncertainty. The honor that descends on me today reflects on all of the Club's members. The sun doesn't shine just for itself. It gives warmth. It burns. It consumes everything around it. This metaphoric language can give you a faint idea of what my role is among you. The Executive Committee's report ends with these words: 'The last thought we wish to offer is that man must explore himself—his goals and values— as much as the world he seeks to change. The dedication to both tasks must be unending. The crux of the matter is not only whether the human species will survive, but even more whether it can survive without falling into a state of worthless existence.'[19] That's quite a program. The task of changing mankind belongs to elevated spirits, to stars—such as ourselves—whose light burns with a pure brilliance. We're at a watershed where the mere language of statistics, the sheer poetry of numbers, cannot suffice to change humanity. The warning is sounded by the prophecies concerning the limits to growth, of arable

---

19. Meadows et al. 197.

land, of the atmosphere, of natural resources. Their echo strangely recalls the warnings of Malthus.[20] And yet the earth continues to revolve. Is it heading for suicide? At each stage, people adapt to their situation. To be sure, the human drama consists of the limits and the possibilities of continued growth. In the end, it's a problem of space. We're worrying ourselves over tomorrow. Worrying kills. Prescience stifles. The revision of values that we dream of is more than just a problem of redeveloping space. Eminent Colleagues, permit me to offer some preliminary remarks, carefully phrased. Our space is so polluted that words have lost their true meaning.

"No equivocation among *savants*. Various well-meaning thinkers around the world have developed a formulation that leads us dangerously astray. I have in mind Herbert Marcuse's *One-Dimensional Man*.[21] No intellectual today can accept the scientistic sophism that encloses us in the circuit of production and consumption, the basis of our alienation, and that means looking at things with blinders on, falling back into the very inadequacies that our Club's mission is to transcend. In

20. The English economist Thomas Malthus (1766–1834) calculated that population growth would inevitably outstrip available resources.

21. The German American philosopher Herbert Marcuse's influential 1964 book criticizes both capitalism and communism for repressing individuality in favor of a totalizing ideology.

place of a one-dimensional space, I propose that we substitute pluridimensional space, composed of many superimposed strata. On top of the circuit of production and consumption we can impose the circuit of sex and consumption, which belongs to a different hierarchy of values. This second circuit so haunts our space that we're unable to perceive the true scale of values. I bring forward as examples the following magazines, displayed on newsstands in NEW YORK, MONTREAL, and so on:

DUDE
ALL MAN
SENSUOUS
WILDCAT
FOR MEN ONLY
SIR
MR.
PLAYBOY
MADAME
MALADE
SEXTUS
SEXE FOU
SEXPRESS ("The most popular whore in town. A breast")
ECSTASY
LESBO
SEXTRA
PARTNERS
SEXY
SECRET
ELLE

LUI
MASCULIN
POSES D'ART
NYMPHO
MIDNIGHT
MINUIT ("The Erotic Umbrella")
ENCORE
SEX ALMANAC
PORNO
BISEXUS
CONFIDENCES
INSIDE NEWS
PLAYGIRL
ADAM
GIRLS AROUND THE WORLD
MAN TO MAN
OUI

Not only women but everything has been sexualized to such an extent that today the human species recognizes a third sexual dimension. People speak of 'trisexual man.' This monstrous being, not predicted by any scientific law, defies Science itself! This new 'parameter' of space confronts us with our responsibilities as men of science. It's taking over television, cinema, radio, all the mass media. It's omnipresent. Even its absence is a presence. The number of fatal accidents (both sexual and cardiac) is extraordinary. Statistics indicate that the number of heart attacks has quintupled in two years. Disturbing phenomenon.

"All the same, science shouldn't be disabled in the face of the sudden apparition of the third man. It has to take up the challenge. According to my initial intuitions—the most sublime truths are born from intuition—this third man reveals to us a fundamental tendency of our being. In desiring a woman, a man expresses the (repressed) desire to rejoin his mother's breast, the first, primordial space. The sexual revolution is thus a normal dynamism. So our epoch has better understood this nostalgic attraction than did earlier periods. Some might think it's a matter of giving rein to an unbridled eroticism so as to regain an undifferentiated Nirvana, a space without depth or solidity. Nothing of the sort! Neither a Nirvana dissolving essences, nor primordial undifferentiation, nor an Impersonal or a Universal whose attribute would be nonbeing, an absolute void. On the contrary, there is a plenitude here: plenitude in a primordial location. Imagine a hundred thousand calls being received at the same moment by a single telephone; by a single individual! One would then be in the presence of a totality amid a multiplicity. Multiplicity mastered by unity. Every one of these telephone calls would retain its individuality, and we can understand why *écriture*, gestural literature, whose mission is to express the movement of primordial unity, is the highest and most sublime expression of our connection with this space that is given

individuality by the writer. Gesture incarnates a plenitude, renders it visible, makes it perceivable in a unique
movement.

"Primordial space. Primordial time. Pure rhythm. Dynamism. Vibratory flux and reflux. Our concepts distort
reality when we surround it with Aristotelian categories. Prior to its exteriorization, it is a word folded back
upon itself, a modulation before it exteriorizes itself in
discourse. It's vain to want to give it a fixed present or to
seek a past for it. My eminent colleague Merleau-Ponty
is right when he speaks of time as a pure rapport with
things, having its roots in the present."[22]

"But Giambatista, doesn't this time have its roots in
our parents' past?"[23]

"I admit heredity, Olobrinus. But heredity isn't time.
It is the weight of another that's become present in me.
It isn't a succession of moments. It's true that parents are
pure relation, but it's necessary to abandon our habit-
ual categories. Here space and time become confused.
Rhythms and vibrations. No dimension, no depth. Don't
look for anything but immediacy. Relativity. Duration

---

22. The French philosopher Maurice Merleau-Ponty (1908–61) wrote
extensively about the historical and embodied quality of experience.
23. Here Viko's friend Olobrinus, still on the telephone, interrupts
Viko's imagined acceptance speech in Rome.

that engenders itself. You'll have to accustom yourself, Olobrinus, to this vocabulary, this somewhat strange turn of thought. My colleagues in the Club who listen most attentively to me understand with no difficulty. It's true that I'm addressing myself to *savants*. Hold on. Here's an experience of mastering time tried by a friend of mine, Bernardo, in the south of the land of the Apika.[24] For three months he gave up using his watch, so as to follow only the movements of the sun. After a while, he lost his sense of a week, the month, the year. Only the day remained for him. But what is a day, Olobrinus, in this context? Is it the space contained between dawn and nightfall? Twelve hours or twenty-four—it's an arbitrary choice. The Apika live in their time. They master it. For them, day doesn't come before night, nor night before day. The Inuit live six months without any 'before dawn' or 'after dusk.' I know that ethnocentrist ideology is already raising its defenses. The philosophers Sartre, Buber, Heidegger, Merleau-Ponty will go to war against this thesis. But the decisive arguments? They come from the philosophical systems themselves. They contradict each other. Where is the truth? 'What is

---

24. A tribe in the Amazon.

truth?' Pilate spits out to the One who calls himself the incarnate Truth![25]

"To tell the truth, isn't truth a pure relation with things? Varying according to the angle of vision with which one chooses to consider things? The ethnocentrist ideology has readily convinced people that 'in place of the real world, primitive or mythic thought substitutes an "otherworld," in place of real space, a space that is "vital" and thereby "sacred," in place of real time, a "primordial" time.' But who gets to decide that a certain space is real and another unreal? It's man! Who mixes the two up? It's man! Truth, dear Colleagues, resides in the relational choice.

"The people we deem primitive create their relation to organize their existence in that manner. We 'civilized' people organize ours according to our own criteria. The primitives have their criteria, we have ours. We often behave like the Scholastics who try to defeat Hegelianism or Marxism by hunting for criteria in Thomas Aquinas, instead of refuting Hegel on his own terms.

"Another comparison can show us the extent of the sophistry we are living with. The State locks up certain individuals in institutions called 'insane asylums.' Who

---

25. When Jesus is tried by Pontius Pilate and says that everyone who belongs to the truth hears his voice, Pilate retorts, "What is truth?" and allows him to be crucified (John 18.38).

can tell us the line of demarcation between madness and nonmadness?[26] I'll wager that the entire planet is an insane asylum. The somewhat less crazy abuse the rest.

"Dear eminent Colleagues—dear Olobrinus—it is necessary to revise our values, our scale of values, but first of all, our concepts. The common platform on which to base all dialogue will be settled concepts, accepted by everyone."

26. Here Viko echoes the critique of psychiatry, and of Western rationality in general, by the philosopher Michel Foucault in works such as *Folie et déraison* (1961; *Madness and Civilization*, 1964).

II

One liter. Two liters. I feel my limbs getting heavy, my mind freeing up. What's this I see? A huge ball with tentacles. Smoke and mist are coming out of it. Ants coupled with elephants; the earth fertilizes the clouds. The lion lies down with the jackal; the star with the mole. The furious dazzling light. The buffalo against the bee, the sea against the waves. Giants' blows.

"Now a third liter. The baptism of deliverance from the Elements. Whoever wants to become himself has to pass through this stage."

We're heading down a subterranean corridor that's maybe two hundred meters long. We come to an opening that seems to serve as a junction. The cavern's walls are freshly adorned with human skins. A skull is hung at every meter. Human and animal bones are piled up pell-mell in all four corners of the cavern. The skulls, specially cut and chiseled, serve to hold different kinds of drink. Scepters hang here and there. A serpent slithers along the cavern at a chameleon's pace. A lugubrious silence reigns.

A hand gives me a goblet filled with red liquid.

"Take it and drink. You are one of us."

"No!" I say.

"Take it and drink. You are one of us. When someone comes to this cavern, either they get out or they don't!"

The voices grow menacing. I take the goblet. Since it's been poured, it has to be drunk.[27] I drink it. A nauseating odor fills the whole cavern. High-pitched voices hiss, alternating with lower ones.

> Those who are pulling you into our universe
> Those who bring you into the universe of
> Those who kill us little by little every day
> Those who paralyze our energies for the sake of
> foreigners will die forever from this blood
> you drink.
> Woe to anyone who dares seek us out to serve
> foreign interests.
> A word to the wise!

The voices keep repeating this refrain. Three times. Is this delirium? A hallucination? Then all of a sudden, blinding lights—red, blue, yellow. Complete darkness. A brightly lit red mask spits out flames, followed by two more masks, then three more. All of a sudden, the whole cavern is filled with masks. Then a procession begins, from the cavern back toward the entrance. Two huge masks, held up by who knows what invisible hands, lead the way. I am

---

27. Echoing the proverb "Quand le vin est tiré il faut le prendre" ("Once the wine's been poured, it has to be drunk").

behind, flanked by two of them on each side. Nearing the entrance, the procession turns around and goes back. Then a general spitting out of flames that get more and more intense. Suddenly they go out. The chorus of voices repeats:

> Those who are pulling you into our universe
> Those who bring you into the universe of
> Those who kill us little by little every day
> Those who paralyze our energies for the sake of
>   foreigners will die forever from this blood
>   you drink.
> Woe to anyone who dares seek us out to serve
>   foreign interests.
> A word to the wise!

A hand strikes me another blow.

"Take it and drink. You are one of us from now on."

I grab it with both hands and drink. It puts me into a deep sleep.

A pause.

"Hello, Madame Giambatista!"

"Olobrinus!"

"What's going on? I was on the phone, but I couldn't hear Giambatista's voice any longer. He seems to have hung up!"[28]

---

28. In the original, this paragraph appears to be spoken by Viko's wife, but this seems to be a printer's error.

"Giambatista shuts himself up in his office at five o'clock every day with a gentleman for a work session. It's strictly forbidden to open the door. Wait till they're done."

I'm aching. Light-headed. My shoulders are heavy. I open the window. Scents of spices and wild flowers. Signs of the approach of the African night. The stubbornness of the sun that refuses to sink. In the courtyard the hens, the pigeons run here and there. On the horizon a rainbow catches the last rays of the sun. Starry prism. Orgy of colors. I don't recall anything like it. My mind jumps from one idea to another, like a monkey from branch to branch. Every image holds on to me for a long time, fascinates me. I am ecstatic. One ecstasy follows another, interspersed with intermittent clawing from my cat. Passing in front of the mirror leaning against a wall, I notice my eyes are popping. I don't recognize myself. Hallucinatory reality? I think so. The African is someone who hallucinates. Rachid Boudjedra is right to believe in the value of hallucination, in the value of madness.[29] We Africans, we're crazy people. "A branching madness," "a screaming madness."[30]

---

29. Rachid Boudjedra (b. 1941) is an Algerian poet, novelist, and critic.

30. These phrases are taken, respectively, from the works of the Congolese poet Tchicaya U Tam'si and Césaire and were cited by Ngal in his 1975 essay "Introduction à une lecture d'Epitomé de Tchicaya U Tam'si" ("Introduction to a Reading of Tchicaya U Tam'si's Epitomé"; 529).

Everything's madness. Rhythms. Dances. Phosphorescent madness. African poetry. Collective delirium. Torrent of debauchery. Love of life. Love of love. *Vie en rut*.[31] Continual nightmare. Nocturnal terrors. Diurnal terrors, mixed-up realities. We ourselves are life. Plenitude. The idea of *le néant*—asinine foreign invention![32] Poisonous venom. Distant lands? Realm of ignorance. Nostalgia, our enemy. Presence, our being. Death, our relaxation. Dream, drunkenness, ecstasy. We hate anticipations. Transitions. Arrivals. Departures. Shifting gears. Everything is presence.

"*Chéri*, Olobrinus is on the phone!"

"Ah! What are you going to do, these poor people need support. It's true, I also make use of them. My interests at the Institute are advancing marvelously thanks to them. If friendship, that kind of *détente* between humans, really exists, I have to extend it to them. The Associates! Despite all my reassurances, anxiety always reigns among them. So my power isn't yet sufficiently recognized! The trouble is that in this country, rumors have as much sub-

---

31. "Life in heat," a sarcastic play on the title of a popular romantic song, "La vie en rose."

32. Jean-Paul Sartre emphasized the self's struggle against *le néant* ("nothingness") in his 1943 existentialist magnum opus, *L'être et le néant* (*Being and Nothingness*).

stance as truth. The word on the street has as much impact as the national radio.

"Olobrinus, dear Olobrinus! It's nothing but a mere rumor. The treaty signed between the two countries remains in force. You know, there is a politics of the crow, who screeches his denunciations, and there's that of the mole. I prefer the latter kind. I give you my word; my protection will be enough for you."

"You are adorable, Giambatista! None of the Associates would know how to survive without you. A wave of Africanization is sweeping the country. We're weak. Returning to the country would be the death of us. We can't be reclassified. We're gnawed by worry; it's our daily bread. Our nights are sleepless; sleep is just a memory for us. And yet we've served this country! We should have had the right to a minimum of recognition. You, you are our hope. Our breath of life. Let's look at the problem from a different angle: that of civilization. Civilization with a capital *C*, based in humanist culture, is dying from day to day. We helplessly take part. If this country had just two intellectuals of your caliber, the West would be overjoyed. The entire colony of Assistants thanks you; I'm acting as their spokesman."

"Thank you. But calm yourself. If your anxiety was well founded, why would I be welcoming our new arrival?"

"You well know Bantu logic.[33] I'm wary of it."

"I'm wary too. It's bewildering. I sympathize with you. I'm smugly assisting in the continent's decivilization, baptized with so many names: African Renaissance, *négritude*, and so on. In reality, this has to do with an Africanolatry; that's the best word for it. But believe me, all is not yet lost. The Western cultural centers—backbones of the Africanolators—are gaining ground. They're helping us remember the permanent presence of culture. Otherwise it would take them centuries to raise their languages to the level of 'languages of culture,'[34] I want to say of international languages. Calm yourself. Tell all your colleagues that I'm with you heart and soul. I've already reached the point of putting a stop to three-quarters of . . . Hello? Can you still hear me?"

"For sure! Your words are golden!"

---

33. A nonlinear mode of thought, open to seeming contradictions. During the period of decolonization in the 1950s and 1960s, a number of Central African intellectuals sought alternatives to westernization by exploring the ancestral thought world of the region's Bantu peoples.

34. Referring to "Le français, langue de culture" ("French, Language of Culture"), an essay by Léopold Sédar Senghor that discusses the ongoing value of French for decolonized African writers, as the best language in which to construct "un monde nouveau—celui de l'Homme. Un monde idéal et réel en même temps" ("a new world—that of Man. A world at once ideal and real"; 840).

"Are you really taking them seriously? Today a reform, tomorrow a retreat, contradiction on top of contradiction. In sum, the perfect illustration of Bantu logic. Just when things reach the point of madness—this is the way to put it—when they decree Africanolatry, that's just when they are really occidentalizing themselves. If their children attend schools at the consulates, or French, Belgian, or English schools in Europe, is it insensitivity? naivete? lack of logic? Are the people duping themselves? I don't believe it. This is to say, dear Olobrinus, we have to take things philosophically. As far as I'm concerned, my choice is clear. More precisely, I don't have one at all. A humanist culture—Greco-Roman—seasoned with the erudition that everyone grants me! Where would you have me find a place for it? I believe neither in cross-breeding nor in the integration of cultures. Juxtaposition? Perhaps! But who could marry Cartesian logic to Bantu logic? You don't mix mud with what's clean!"

"Some Third Worlders declare that international capitalism is informing the 'deep nature' of the harvesters of palm nuts in the equatorial forest. Since the social, the cultural, and so forth don't intrude themselves all of a sudden but are already there in the realm of production, don't you believe in the slow death of Bantu culture among those impoverished harvesters?"

"In Marxist-Leninist logic, yes! That's our credo, and that of every cultivated man. Marx, Lenin, Althusser.[35] Our gurus. Yet the rigidity of the model should give us pause. Local heterogeneities often cause unanticipated disruptions. That's what makes me believe in the possibility of the juxtaposition of cultures—in the 'marxization' of Marxism itself today. The parameters proposed by Marx aren't as frozen as certain eager Third Worlders let themselves think. Proof: the multiple readings of Marx. No reader of the author of *Das Kapital* can claim to have said the last word."

"It's always stunning to see the haste with which some people in the Third World canonize Marx and Lenin. I'll bet those guys are turning over in their graves. Just think a bit about the wave of 'bantuization' of Marxism that the continent is experiencing these days."

"The key thing is to expose the kind of lucidity that conceals the refusal to discuss the real problems that the people face. Marxism has become opium just as much as soccer has.[36] A distraction. It's quite an art!"

"Today 'development' means distraction. Politics too has become the art of creating distractions. What is

---

35. Louis Althusser (1918–90) was a leading Marxist philosopher in Paris.

36. Viko applies to Marxism itself the famous assertion by Karl Marx that religion is the opium of the people (Introduction).

the responsibility of the rest of us, intellectuals, in this situation?"

"We play along, mindlessly, stupefied. The gris-gris are given more credit than our intellectuals. And then . . . you have to be wealthy to be considered. Those bourgeois who have arisen out of nothing, who constitute that periphery that Samir Amin talks about.[37] Their assets—Himalayas built up in fifteen years. Philistines. How to get them back? Reverse values, the scale of value? Now they're on the world circuit. The machine runs. The mechanism is implacable: the law of the expanded accumulation of capital. Creation of adequate surplus value. Profit. Need to perpetuate alienated labor. Exploitation. These outcries are those of Herbert Marcuse. The earth can't be saved within the framework of capitalism; the Third World can't be developed according to the capitalist model. The struggle for an extension of the world of beauty, nonviolence, and peacefulness is a political struggle. The insistence on these values, on the restoration of the earth as a human environment, isn't just a romantic, aesthetic, poetic idea that only concerns the privileged; today it's a question of survival. The goal is to achieve well-being through a life freed of fear, of

---

37. Samir Amin (1931–2018) was an Egyptian political scientist who coined the term *Eurocentrism*.

wage slavery, of violence, of the stench and the infernal roar of the industrial capitalist world. It isn't a matter of cloaking outrages in euphemisms, of hiding the misery, of deodorizing the stench, of prettying up the prisons, the banks, the factories; it isn't a matter of purifying existing society but of replacing it."

"I can't see you, but I imagine it's Herbert Marcuse who's speaking like this through your mouth!"

"He's one of *les maîtres* who have marked me. But he has evolved, you know. Just like a Benedictine monk thinks of the word of his God by reference to the Bible, I too have my gods. They have names: Marx, Lenin, Althusser, Sartre, Marcuse. In life, everyone has his god."

"Don't your gods seem to live in the sanctuary of books?"

"Marx and Lenin aren't some bookish universe. They are the engine of history. Their doctrine is, I should say. The progress of history is inconceivable without them."

Our discussion goes on. Jumping around. The problem of *écriture* returns. My fame. The creative spirit. The material. Its resistances. Form. Style. Dreams. Fantasies. Hallucinations. Art. Creative labor. The struggle of genius to impose form on marble. Michelangelo's chisel drawing Moses out of the void. The artist is god. He conceives, he projects, he inscribes his fantasies onto the white page. He carves them in stone; he transposes them into music. He gives form to the material. A demi-urge . . . I feel the passion for writing resurface; I break off the conversation with Olobrinus.

Ideas swarm within my head. Confrontation with phantasms. Body to body. All at once, images seem to flow in my discourse. Others hold back and stay on the threshold. My paralysis seems to be cured. But why this precipitation of images? Do they all want to be received in a single stream, without waiting to be put in order? I feel as if there are two contradictory powers within myself. One sets the phantasms free, the other holds them back. The first wants to lodge all of them in the flux and reflux of phrases. The second is opposed to this and wants to spread them out, one after the other. Some of the phantasms are pure rhythms and vibrations; as hard as I concentrate, I can't manage to settle them down. Have I woken up, or am I dreaming? No, I'm completely lucid. Having by now reached the end of my initiation, I should have been capable of creating the dreamed-of gestural literature. Have I violated some interdiction? Perhaps! But who will let me know? The secret is absolute. Indiscretion, fatal. No, this is just a feeling.

"Hello, Niaiseux!"

"*Maître!*"

"You're always so quick to recognize le *Maître*'s voice! How are things going?"

41

"The silent treatment is working beautifully. He can't find anyone to talk to at the Institute. Even Malawi, who he's always talking with, seems to have turned his back on him. You know that Malawi, that little snake in the grass, doesn't lack ambition. He's no happier with X's scholarly success, anyway, than with yours. The Blacks are all the same. They have trouble stomaching their neighbor's success. Don't you recall all the curses that the village women launch against their neighbors when their hens are cackling in their pens after laying their eggs? It's as if we've heard him whispering bitter words!"

"Malawi's problem is the lack of any opening to the outside. He's enclosed within a specialty without a breath of fresh air. I feel sorry for him; but that doesn't keep us from making use of him. One always makes alliance against a common enemy. You'll get him on your side with a meal of mwambe.[38] I always invest a quarter of my salary in the dinners I give. Tomorrow, it's Sirbu's turn to be welcomed. You'll be one of us anyway."

"*Maître*, all of this is perfect. But you'll have to defeat this snake in the grass by asserting yourself through a series of publications. The illusory credit that he enjoys with the authorities stems from the impression he gives of publishing a great deal."

---

38. A hearty chicken stew, the Congolese national dish.

"An illusion that won't last long at all. My star cannot permit such subordination, especially to a Black. The delay in my publications is only temporary. The *décollage*, as the psychoanalysts say, won't be long now.[39] I've long been assembling an anthology of texts on literary creation. Selections from all the geniuses humanity has produced. The phenomenon of osmosis is bound to kick in. From one genius to another, needless to say. One genius heroically identifying with another can produce miracles. You know how Freud came to realize himself as at once both a poet and a great writer? By his heroic identification with Goethe, through symbolic filiation with Goethe's creative genius. It's a well-known anecdote. At age thirty-nine, on the occasion of his journey to Naples, the author of *Elective Affinities* rediscovers or revives his inspiration and his style. In the same way, it's at age thirty-nine that Freud finds himself, on the occasion of his first voyage to Italy. It's necessary to have an identification, a symbolic filiation, with a brilliant creator."

"Hugo did the same thing in identifying with Chateaubriand."[40]

"Indeed! And yet identification isn't just imitation."

---

39. In Freudian thought, creativity has to achieve a *décollage*, or liftoff, like a bird or airplane taking flight.

40. At age fourteen, the future novelist Victor Hugo vowed to become "Chateaubriand ou rien" ("Chateaubriand or nothing"; Hugo 297).

"But is it possible across cultures, between geniuses who belong to different cultures? Can an African genius really identify symbolically with a European one?"

"Would you perhaps be calling into question, for the very first time, my humanist culture that affiliates itself with the Great Europeans? Still, your question is worth posing. But to dispel any uncertainty: my die is cast. Whatever could shackle my European filiation is completely neutralized in the very instant when I talk with you. It's one and the same thing to liberate my genius and to liberate the European discourse confined within me. It's no longer a question of a '*décollage*.' Every Icarus owes his wings to a Daedalus."

"*Maître*, how could you think such a thing of Niaiseux? Don't you know that I've devoted an unconditional cult to your person? Everyone in the Institute has to act the same way. If the sun shines today, it is thanks to you."

"I'm not accusing you of anything, Niaiseux. Your question is appropriate. Even geniuses need dialogue now and then to refine their thought. I can declare to you that I am 'lifting off' today, like Marcel Proust's young Bergotte.[41]—'To mount the skies it is not necessary to

---

41. Bergotte is a great but unappreciated writer in Proust's *À la recherche du temps perdu* (*In Search of Lost Time*), here described in the second volume, *À l'ombre des jeunes filles en fleurs* (554–55; *Within a Budding Grove*; 175–76).

have the most powerful of motors, one must have a motor which, instead of continuing to run along the earth's surface, intersecting with a vertical line the horizontal which it began by following, is capable of converting its speed into lifting power. Similarly, the men who produce works of genius are not those who live in the most delicate atmosphere, whose conversation is the most brilliant or their culture the most extensive, but those who have had the power, ceasing suddenly to live only for themselves, to transform their personality into a sort of mirror, in such a way that their life, however mediocre it may be socially and even, in a sense, intellectually, is reflected by it, genius consisting in reflecting power and not in the intrinsic quality of the scene reflected. The day on which the young Bergotte succeeded in showing to the world of his readers the tasteless household in which he had spent his childhood, and the not very amusing conversations between himself and his brothers, was the day on which he rose above the friends of his family, more intellectual and more distinguished than himself; they in their fine Rolls-Royces might return home expressing due contempt for the vulgarity of the Bergottes; but he, in his modest machine which had at last "taken off," soared above their heads.'

"Brilliant Proust! He's right. I'm in front of that mirror today. I see myself reflected in it. My creativity has never been so ready to take on the wings of Icarus as at this moment. What I've called paralysis is nothing more than an incubation. A long incubation! Finally the mystery has been solved! I taste success. I revel in it, in the thousands of readers who circle around like a swarm of bees, who attack my text. My *œuvre*. Comprehensible and incomprehensible. Overflowing with meaning. Every bee adds his own meaning to it, sucks its nectar. Plenitude. I am inexhaustible. My name sails through the universe. Studied, discussed. Subject of memoirs and dissertations. Interviewed on television. Sought out for autographs. Cited in all the anthologies, along with other geniuses. Dialoguing with other geniuses. Idol of the young. Brought up in every intellectual conversation."

"*Maître*, your first two essays and your collections of poetry already rank you among the world's most famous classics."

"Essayist—not enough. Essayist, novelist, poet, yes! At last I can count myself among the polyvalent geniuses. The Napoleon of African letters. Of the whole world. Radiance. Brio. Black poetry. No—poetry of mankind. There's nothing black about me except my skin. My *œuvre* consecrates me for immortality. A laureate's immortality? No, immortality's seed. Malraux creates the higher world of art in order to escape the void; an image powerful enough to reduce the void to nothingness. My monument—my unique *chef-d'œuvre*—is its own immortality. Plenty of geniuses—false geniuses, to tell the truth—are preoccupied with the survival of their *œuvre*. The true genius doesn't worry, since he is already an eternal presence in the world: immortality's seed."

"These words are so novel, *Maître*, that I fear they will get lost. We need a Plato to reproduce them. Having died, Socrates survives himself; your words fly away. *Verba volant.* The telephone suppresses all distance, annihilates space, but it doesn't record what you say. I have a very short memory . . . There are clever technicians who can install for us a combination telephone and tape recorder for your words."

"Thanks to the telephone, my words escape from space. If you fix them on reels of tape, you bring them again under the law of space. If the human being can't escape it, the genius would be well advised to find a substitute that can allow him to master it, to find a way to battle against space. Just as gestural literature has to reveal us to ourselves, the telephone's operation allows us to discover our capacity to overcome every obstacle."

"Your genius overcomes every suggestion and every objection!"

"My dear Niaiseux, I am at a crossroads. I see my *œuvre* exposed to the public, definitively detached from myself. A genius, you know, has his moments of anguish, like Christ in the Garden of Gethsemane. He sees his *œuvre* confront reactions, assessments, critiques. Or what's worse, the public's indifference. There is such a thing as the unrecognized genius! Either because the age isn't yet ready to welcome him, or because, having understood, it rejects him."

"But that isn't your case. You're far beyond the stage of public recognition."

"I sacrifice on the altar of creation. You don't know how much this costs me. Solitude. Alone in this adventure. Broken up, torn apart. As in giving birth. Do you know the mother's anguish in childbirth? Ours is the uncertainty of the frailty of beauty. Creation's paths are slippery. Snares can trap the writing, turn it into a mere shadow. On finishing the last page of their work, how many geniuses haven't sung Desnos's lovely poem:

> I've had such dreams of you
> I've gone so far, talked so much,
> Loved your shadow so much
> That there's nothing left of you.
> I'm left a shadow among the shadows,
> A hundred times more shadowy than the shadow,
> To be the shadow that will come and go in your
>   somnolent life.[42]

---

42. The concluding lines of "J'ai tant revé de toi" ("I've Had Such Dreams of You"; 85), said to be the last poem by the French surrealist Robert Desnos (1900–45).

"That's our condition, my dear Niaiseux . . . Handed over to the fate of creation . . ."

The other phone rings. It's Castino Paqua on the line. Here I am with two phones, one at my left ear, the other at my right. I'm in the middle, like an umpire in a tennis match. More like an arbitrator. Castino Paqua is another of those creatures who devote a cult to me that is more calculated than genuine. She knows my power, that I can fix everything for the Associates. A lighter character, more playful, completely saucy. She reads a lot. Totally full of ideas soaked up from *Emmanuelle*,[43] she thinks she has a vocation. Having sacrificed at Mario's altar, she wants to be the missionary of the gospel that is bound to revolutionize traditional love and expose the traps of feeling in love.

She is calling to fill me in on the latest spreading of local rumors.

"Do you know what they're saying about you?"

"Still?"

"Yes, of course! If there ever stop being rumors, that'll be the end of everything. No more breathing. Not another look. No more glances. No more sniffing. It'll be paradise!"

---

43. An erotic novel (1967) by Emmanuelle Arsan, in which the avid Emmanuelle is instructed in free love by Mario, an aging gay voyeur.

"I can't wait to learn . . ."

"*Maître*, Denos's poem is exquisitely beautiful. Could you repeat it for me? I've got a pencil all ready to take it down."

"You can find it in the collection of Desnos's poetry, page 250."

"They're saying that you've been seen at Catholic Mass. The Althusserian, the Leftist, is now worshipping at the YANKEE altar! Paying court to the capitalists . . . The humanism of refusal! . . ."

"You're shocked? This is just for the sake of defending immediate interests. Tactics, that's something you still have to learn."

"Doesn't it seem as though Desnos is setting his earlier work at nothing?"

"That's why *écriture* has to be a showplace of shadows. Paradox? No. Shadows of what they are not."

"But not everyone understands it that way. A lot of people are dropping you. Opportunism is getting mixed up with the true defense of interests."

She hangs up. I try calling her back. The phone rings, but she realizes it's me trying to recapture her. I break off. My genius isn't one that lets itself be moved by the statements of a girl. What little I get out of it is still an advantage for her. Some information now and then. Not to be neglected. Everything counts.

I hang up the other line too. Niaiseux is losing himself in more and more stupid exclamations.

Outside the sun isn't setting. A cool breeze whips across my face. I close the window. I'm always afraid of a recurrence of bronchitis. In delicate health; the least imprudence costs me dearly. I'm still recovering from an illness that could have taken my life. The doctor says: "No more alcohol. No more cigarettes. No more . . ." But that's suicide! He wants me to get treatment abroad. Going away! That would mean a considerable delay in my work. On the other hand, there'd be an advantage: contacts with foreign colleagues. Ones who know me, ones who don't. Increase the diameter of the circle of my reputation. Slip in my visiting card here and there. My CV is already bulging. My research in categories: 1: Books. 2: Edited volumes. 3: Works in press. 4: Completed works not yet legally deposited.[44] 5: Completed works in the process of being deposited. 6: Works nearing completion. 7: Works in progress. 8: Works at the planning stage. 9: Works at the preplanning stage. 10: Works about to take off. 11: Works moved ahead by the sheer force of desire.

---

44. A copy of every book published in France has to be sent to the Bibliothèque Nationale de France (National Library of France).

12: Works ready to be delivered. 13: Essays. 14: Cowritten essays. 15: Essays completed and legally deposited. 16: Essays completed but not yet deposited. 17: Essays in press. 18: Essays that have merely been conceived. 19: Essays on the back burner. 20: Creative essays. 21: Scientific essays. 22: Sociological essays. 23: Literary-critical essays. 24: Miscellaneous essays . . . Such polyvalent talent! Such pluridimensional talent! I read the reactions in the faces of everyone I pass: "He writes with equal facility on literary criticism, on economics, on anthropology, on theology, on linguistics, on graphology." I see people give way before me and lower their heads with veneration. "The *savant* is going by. He doesn't speak much. He is sententious. Dry, sober in his speech. Head slightly inclined. Hair not too well combed."

My writings are making an impression. The key? References. *The Encyclopaedia Britannica* makes an effect. Brilliantly used method: works cited but never read. Book reviews in the journal *Culture et développement*, precious instrument of mystification!

"Hello?"

"Niaiseux on the line!"

"Ah! Good time for you to call. Here's an interesting idea. We have Chinese and Japanese scholars at the Institute. Suppose I get my recent essays translated and publish them, without mentioning 'Translated into

Chinese by Sing-chiang Chu' and 'Translated into Japanese by Hitachi Huyafusia-yama.' Just signing them 'GIAMBATISTA VIKO.' That would clearly impress the public: the author knows both those languages. What do you think?"

"The idea seems enticing. Others have already managed to do this. Deontologically speaking, it isn't intellectual dishonesty; you're just benefitting from services rendered by others!"

"No *savant* today can get by without a knowledge of several international languages. To know English—not to mention French, that goes without saying—Spanish, Russian, that's good. Japanese, that's even better; Chinese is ten times better, since the future, the key to the future, belongs to Asia, especially to China. The Westerners are terribly afraid of the Yellow Peril, but how long can they hope to hold out? They know how to combat yellow fever, arrest its spread. But they can't do a thing against the Yellow Peril.

"Translations! That will pad the list of my publications. Just one false note: the novel that's underway. The various lines I've written so far don't seem to do justice to my genius. A style at the crossroads of many contradictory tendencies: the incantatory, the learned, the moving, the oracular. Sometimes flashing out, glittering, sometimes deconstructed. Abrupt opacities here, profound transparencies there. An internal, obsessional discourse, dissolved in an indescribable jumble of times and confusion of perspectives. Punctuation? Don't even mention it! Failure is looming on the horizon."

"*Maître*, that word should never come out of your mouth. I see this rather as a sign of genius. A way of getting out of the dry academicism of the African novel."

"Maybe! Might such contradictory tendencies in a single text lead to the destruction of that kind of novel? Celebrate its burial? But one thing bothers me—the troubling cohabitation of heterogenous elements."

"All you're doing is complaining. But wouldn't it be appropriate to initiate yourself into the science of *écriture*?"

"That's an idea! The initiate is an Other. He is one who has progressed from ignorance to knowledge, to true *savoir*. The *scienza nuova* I'm seeking. Our culture— the Western, I mean—no longer has a sense for initiation. Nobody believes in it anymore. It's only the West that finds itself in this situation. It exists almost everywhere else. Do you think that a Westerner who'd go to a foreign society to have himself initiated would really be advancing science? The new science would have to be in effect a new state of consciousness that would inform the connection between beings and things. But would its realization lead to personal fulfillment? Would an unbelieving Westerner be capable of such a metamorphosis? How could he hope to achieve such a state of grace?"

"Looking at things that way, such a gesture would only be a masquerade."

"So it's impossible to achieve this other 'I'! For an initiation is a passage from nature to culture. The equation is as follows: a passage from ignorance to knowledge equals a passage from nature to culture. Outside the West, the initiate arrives at being—to discover the deep meaning of things; to read beyond what the senses perceive; to comprehend the cosmic connections between human existence and man's interior dimension."

"An initiation can only function within the same culture."

"The ethnologists who bribe these African or Amazonian tribes with a bit of salt, of money, are committing a sacrilegious act that will finally lead them to madness. It's this contradiction at the heart of the sacrilegious gesture that precludes a personal realization."

"But that shouldn't put you off, *Maître*. Isn't life a contradiction? Just look at the mass of African intellectuals who are aid workers in their own country and set themselves up well in the process. Of course, the analogy isn't exact, but it's suggestive."

"When it has to do with a desacralized society, contradiction can lead to self-realization. But what kind of self-realization? Materially, sure, but that doesn't get very far. That's what we see with quite a few intellectuals in the West. I'm very uneasy. For every intellectual is in somewhat the same situation . . ."

A moment of silence between Niaiseux and me . . . I seem to be recalling, as in a dream, the menacing echo of certain words:

> Those who are pulling you into our universe
> Those who bring you into the universe of
> Those who kill us little by little every day
> Those who paralyze our energies for the sake of
>   foreigners will die forever from this blood
>   you drink.
> Woe to anyone who dares seek us out to serve
>   foreign interests.
> A word to the wise!

"*Maître*, the problem seems extremely serious to me: to get beyond the simple contradiction classically overcome through the synthesis of a thesis and its antithesis. The coexistence of different cultures within a single individual is a constant source of stress. One is no longer 'one' but 'two,' 'three,' 'heterogeneous.' If you want to plunge into *écriture*, it will be the discourse of the 'two' or the 'three.' A heterogeneous text. Fragments. Detached. Unconnected. Several voices at the same time. The text appears more like a matrix for producing promiscuous elements. The flow of phrases yields surprising effects. Hallucinatory words. Phantasms. Shadowy corners. An overpowering explosion of artifice. Rhetoric. A choreographic effect. Sonorous. Sticky. Agglutinated. Agglutinating. A graphic music. Rhythmic. Verbal orgies. The *décollage* is achieved. But the result? There it is."

"Really, there are diverse discourses within me, none of them fully mastered. A sign that I'm torn in spite of myself. Several of them seem to speak at the same time. Perhaps one doesn't renounce one's mother with impunity. Literally as well as figuratively. This is my case. You know that my people call me 'a White.' We have nothing in common but our skin. On the cultural level, an unbridgeable abyss separates us. Only biological solidarity still connects us. But what is biology in the face of the cultural? We'd have to encounter ourselves again in nature; a return to nature for me. A countercultural progress. But becoming rooted again—is that possible? If so, how? Africa is deracinated in me. It's been killed in the egg. The West has been planted there. Is there any way to leap across the bridge between the two realms?

"Poets have succeeded through the magic of words. But they remain drawn to an elsewhere. That's what defines them. If that draw were to disappear, there wouldn't be any more tension—or any more poetry. Jean Amrouche, eternally torn between ascent and descent.[45] The ascent: to mythic ancestors. The descent: into the present, the future. He wanted to have both at once. He was looking for his name: 'My name is Man. I know it, but Man is always one man, the man who I am. At the moment, I feel that I'm condemned to difference, to an irreducible and disquieting singularity. . . . The field of battle is within myself: there isn't a shred of my spirit and my soul that doesn't belong at one and the same time to the two camps that are killing them. I'm Algerian, and I believe myself completely French.' We are a battlefield. Writing is where this battle finds expression, indeed, a place of reconciliation with ourselves. For the quest is never satisfied, because the battle has never ended. A style always subjected to torture: our proper name and our identity."

"Is a choice perhaps still possible?"

"Illusory."

---

45. Jean Amrouche was a francophone Algerian poet (1906–62). His *Journal, 1928–1962* has entries that resonate with Viko's preoccupations. "Je ne suis pas de la race de ceux qui font carrière. Mes frères sont Nerval et Rimbaud" ("I am not of the race of those who build a career. My brothers are Nerval and Rimbaud"; 77). "Devenir français . . . est toujours à imiter. . . . Au final, c'est se condamner à ne pas être" ("To become French . . . is always to imitate. . . . In the end, it's to condemn oneself to not be"; 315).

"Like everything in life. But deceptively soothing."

These last words of Niaiseux's descend like a veil onto my spirit. Night approaches. The sun's last rays give a pallor to the horizon. The struggle between day and night seems to have been won by the latter. Struggle between Angel and Man.

III

Sitting at my table, window curtains drawn open, I contemplate the chickens who stubbornly refuse to go into the coop. One cock dominates. The only male among the twenty who make up my household, he too seems to have a special mission. The hens approach, in a circle, joining together. He mounts one, then another. Mythic gesture. Ritual. Seemingly free, but beyond time. Eternal. Present in the intensity of the present. Ruled by no law. I'm thinking about Castino Paqua. Shouldn't she "scientifically" observe these creatures, follow their example? The cock enters his domain without partiality, without apprehension, hoping to find new sources of interest there, and with a desire to succeed. But isn't it unjust of me to ascribe such ideas to the poor girl? Her beloved Emmanuelle says: Liberty is the opposite of ignorance. Then the colony before me is a realm of the ignorant . . .

"Hello—Climax here!"

"Greetings, you old savage. How are you doing? Sirbu is with us. What luck for the Institute!"

"Yes, I know, it's a piece of luck. We'll have to exploit it fully. He's a guy with a lot of ideas; we have to know how to make use of him."

"The arrangements are made. My German isn't good; I'm thinking of entrusting him with the translation of several of my articles and essays."

"Great idea! I could take charge of the Portuguese. What do you think about that?"

"Perfect. I greatly esteem this valuable mode of collaboration at its true worth. It's possible with you others; but with the Blacks! . . ."

"That's what we've all noticed. In this whole country there aren't two people of your temperament. They talk a lot; they want big positions."

"Blacks are sons of the goddess Jealousy. For myself, I don't want to keep on working among them. I'm a French official in terms of my cultural and scientific activities; I dream of the day when I'll find myself back in Paris. Like Lucien de Rubempré,[46] everything in me calls out for Paris. Do you understand my martyrdom? Your presence is a comfort to me."

"I hope our departure won't be a catastrophe!"

"You are one of the few who comprehend my situation, the phantasm that pursues me night and day. The singularity of my experience translates into the malaise that gnaws at my life like a cancer."

---

46. A protagonist in Balzac's *La comédie humaine* who comes from the provinces to conquer Parisian society.

"One instinctively understands you. Your discourse is ours. Mirror of the West that recognizes itself in it."

"You're a true poet, Climax!"

"We're giving you and your African colleagues every opportunity to give birth to this discourse. Some people want to counter it with a hypothetical African discourse, erected in an effort to dereify the West's ethnocentric gaze. A vulgar absurdity. An attempt doomed to fail in the egg. Could they manage it? On what basis? We've given you everything, even the ability to dispute us."

"Climax, I beg you! . . ."

"When I say 'you,' I'm not including *you* in this admittedly ambiguous pronoun. I get annoyed and I protest against this desire to elevate myths, legends, and African tales to the level of scientific discourse. They combat us with a system of immutable beliefs, opposing us with a hypothetical Africanness or African personality. Pamphlets, manifestos, and essays are flooding the market. We magnanimously throw open the doors of our publishing houses for this twaddle that drags the West through the mud, insulted, trampled on. Our discourse, put into question with an immeasurable flippancy, is supposed to await its relief by a properly African scientific practice? This new ideology is a counter-ideology. But people forget that science isn't ideology's daughter."

"Your rhetoric is violent enough to topple mountains. The Africans could retort: Your strongly felt need to primitivize the life that your hyperscience dessicates is itself born from contact with Africa. You confine man on ruinous conceptual reservations: essence, existence, reason, and so on. Man needs to be decolonized and then colonized in the West. You've learned decolonization from us; as for colonization, Africa generously leaves that to you. Stripped of his wealth, man can recover it in the continent that has remained virgin."

"I'll admit that we give the African a miraculous weapon for the uncontrolled and abusive employment of a poorly defined vocabulary.[47] Metaphors should never mask the truth. They give off too much romantic and Rousseauean perfume."

"All in all, it's a trap. Both the Westerners and the Africans unwittingly fall into it. The former mix up literature and reality; the latter feel themselves at ease as

---

47. Alluding to Césaire's surrealist poem *Les armes miraculeuses* (*Miraculous Weapons*; *Complete Poetry* 62–305), which features strings of disconnected phrases, "les enfantillages de l'alphabet des spasmes" ("the childish tricks of the alphabet of spasms"; 106; 107) from "la berceuse congolaise que les soudards m'ont désapprise" ("the Congolese cradle-song that the old troopers untaught me").

though they're in their natural element. Thus the myth of primitivity reinforces their belonging to a universe in which the sacred and the profane are intertwined, in a totalizing vision. But one thing disturbs me. Despite the steamroller of colonization, of Western science and technology, African voices still retain more than enough power to nourish our dreams, our passions. Filled with a haunting presence, they unsettle the most lucid minds of our times. Is it necessary to cross out with a stroke of the pen those mythic personages, their cries, their tears, and their laughter, which are like a recovered childhood for modern man? They come to draw us out of our solitude, placing us in a network of exchange, of communication with the universe."

"I'll allow a methodological perspective that teaches us to regard the Other with a bit of love."

"You believe in an exchange between civilizations?"

"At the methodological level, yes."

"But how can you conceive a methodological efficacy without a genuine celebration of the world through a harmonic range like that of Africa? According to that logic—your logic—Africa merely remains an object to serve your interests. Does love still have any place in enslavement?"

"You're telling me that everything is finally nothing more than egotistical self-interest, including our own view of ourselves. Love exists in the paradise of myth; it's no more than a shadow down here with us."

"But what is the boundary between the shadow and the reality? Whoever could tell you that is really smart. What is the boundary between life and death, between the one of us who is 'wise' and the one who is 'demented'? Between the normal and the abnormal? Shadows begin where reality ends, death where life ends; the *sapiens*—the normal—is where the 'demented,' the abnormal, begins."

"That's to say that love begins where egotistical self-interest ends."

I hang up. The discussions with my friends take us out of time. We hang on the telephone without realizing that time is passing, helped along by the sunset's astonishing complicity. Talking on all these telephone lines at once puts me into a theatrical scene of which I'm the master of ceremonies, the center on whom everything converges, the mental nucleus resembling that primordial space-time continuum that I dream of translating into my novel. Each of my friends is like an atom spinning around me. I bring time to a halt. I annihilate space. Me.

A clock that runs without the hours of the day going by. A train in motion without burning through space. My house, this dreamed-of primordial space. One doesn't go there: one is present. It isn't five o'clock, six o'clock. No. Time stands still. I am time. I am space. Having conquered time, I build pure rhythms on its rubble! A mad dance. Towering space of duration. Archipelago of well-being. Of science. Well-being and science: brother and sister. Harbor. Fountain of youth. Delightful pleasures.

IV

The door opens.

"Your head is buried in your arms!"

"Oh, *chérie*! The birth isn't happening. The intuition is there. Dazzling. A singular opportunity; I have to give it form. I know my heroine's physical characteristics, her desires, her character. I see her before me, shining with life and color. I wish you could see her in the radiance of her beauty, her intelligence. Open your eyes. Look. She appears out of an invisible vision. I'd like my *écriture* to shake her, to jostle her. The role of fiction—to give her life. If only she'd cease being a lackey of my dreams. Listen: she's speaking to me, you speak, speak to her. Alert, vivacious, needy. Lovely *coiffeur*. Perfumed. Ready for the ceremony . . ."

"What ceremony?"

"Surely a reception?"

"What is she saying?"

"Nothing!"

"What kind of shoes is she wearing?"

"High heels, brown-beige!"

"Is anybody with her?"

"No doubt her husband! He seems terribly jealous. He doesn't leave her for a second. There they are at the reception. In an embassy. *Le Tout* . . . is there.[48] People greet her with respect. Lingeringly. That doesn't seem to please her husband too much. People turn around; people follow her. Radiant sun."

"Whatever is well conceived presents itself clearly. Translated into art: what has been experienced is easily expressed. As one lives, so one writes. Not: as one writes, one lives."

"Your intuition is distressing; it troubles me!"

"I'm only expressing a truism. The writing is the man. As the saying goes, *Le style, c'est l'homme.*[49] One can't develop a text in parallel with one's life. Writing follows the man."

"As the man is, so is the writing. That doesn't mean that art imitates life. Well, in a certain sense. Even the most imaginary works, those most remote from our daily lives, are still a kind of imitation in some way. To put it clearly: in art, emotional duplicity, insincerity, leads directly to an impasse. Many people are drawn to writing by snobbism, by the taste of the day, what's in the air, what's interesting. That's what leads to artistic paralysis. It's a matter of being authentic—ah! the word is

---

48. Evoking the common expression *le Tout-Paris* (everyone who is anyone).

49. "Style is the man," an aphorism from the Comte de Buffon's 1753 *Discours sur le style* (*Discourse on Style*; 18).

hackneyed!—as much in life as in art. Writing doesn't hold second place, juxtaposed with life. It receives its true being from life. It's in that sense that we say style is the man. Just look at Malraux's *œuvre*. The author of *La condition humaine* speaks about death with an exemplary sincerity, in book after book.[50] Not that Malraux had experienced death; but he had dramatic experience *of* it. He didn't just know it from books. In the situations he reports, death insinuated itself into his being when he confronted it during the era of the Resistance, later through illness. The only way to continue to live seemed to him to be by writing. That's why *The Obsidian Head*, *Lazarus*, and *The Unreal* are books that have the quality of testimony."

"It seems as if we hear Solomon speaking through your mouth. You move among these concepts with a totally biblical wisdom and spontaneity. Your words take hold as much by their justice as by their solemnity. I imbibe them like a soothing drink. *In ore infantium sapientia.*[51] Truth comes from children, because they're pure. Your words are pure. Bare. It's the artist in you that's

---

50. André Malraux (1901–76) wrote novels about his early adventures in Indochina and his anti-fascist activities during the Spanish Civil War and World War II, as well as works on the theory of art. His 1933 novel *La condition humaine* (*Man's Fate*) concerns a failed Communist rebellion in Shanghai.

51. "Out of the mouths of babes comes wisdom" (Psalm 8.2).

speaking. You carry creative hopefulness within you. You've got it right: that's the source of art. We women are artists through motherhood. Our children are artistic masterpieces, because we carry deep within ourselves the hope of motherhood. A woman who lacks that could well find all the resources of intelligence, imagination, money blocked; she'd never gain access to the masterpiece of nature that is giving birth. Art too is an *œuvre* of childbirth."

"First one has to foster people who believe in the hope for innovation. It isn't the public's judgment but hope that causes a child or a work of art to be born. The public only takes note of it. Plenty of people are paralyzed by the idea of the public's judgment. A great mistake. Art is above and beyond the public."

"So the public responds to another, superimposed, notion: that of communication. Creation as such doesn't attract the public, no matter what some authors say."

"But words form a significant universe!"

"I don't disagree with that. It's another dimension, if you like, of the *œuvre*. It's a question of logical priority. If you get fixated on the problem of communication, you won't produce a word; your novel won't advance an inch. Anyway, why are you so concerned with the public? Once you let go of a work, it no longer belongs to you. It's a field opened up for the critical swine to root around in. It becomes a citadel to assault. The lovely heroine you're so ecstatic about becomes your double, according to some critics, or the source of your alienation according to others . . . Lots of them will undress her, dress her again differently; will torture her, proposition her, prostitute her. You'll no longer recognize her. That's what the public is. Indiscretion. Stripping naked. Immodesty. Those are the zones the public loves to move in. In the face of this kind of masochistic iconoclasm, you'll no longer recognize your daughter *œuvre*. The public keeps chiseling. Carves the marble its own way. Does a '*striptease*' on your work. You'll find yourself assaulted on all sides. Orphan. Widow. Husband. Lover. Cuckold. Shunned by some, hated by the rest."

"Is it still worth the trouble to write, if this is the situation of the work and the experience of writing? It's enough if the work doesn't disown you."

"The experience of writing is like that of fatherhood or motherhood. Today you give a child to the world. When it grows up, as a young man, a young woman, your child may refuse to acknowledge you. After all the sweating, the tears, to bring the kid up! We don't raise them for us but for themselves. Like the proverb says: 'As long as you can, keep having children; you'll find one of them who will acknowledge you.' It's the same with writing. Produce as much as possible. One of your works will make you what you hope to be. What are you thinking of calling your novel? "The Passion of . . ."—wouldn't that do best for the title?"

"Too religious! It would evoke the passion of Christ, or I don't know what Catholic saint . . . The title has to be evocative. Suiting the central design of my research. Some other historical personage might do the trick."

"But for now, the title seems secondary. The key thing is for you to 'lift off.'"

As she's talking with me, my eyes fall on a framed photo of the castle at the Principality of Monaco. Souvenir of a visit together with a student from Gabon. Edifice all lit up. Red, white. Yacht. French flag on a gilded pole mounted on a base. My companion and I were sitting in the restaurant adjoining the casino. A girl in front of us. Alone. Ah! Lise! She doesn't soften. Image of incommunicability between races, civilizations. New interpellation.[52] New challenge.

"Don't you think we need to invent a literature that can protect writers from the public? One that would make the public take part in writing the text? An open literature format, like the open-access programs on the

---

52. In "Idéologie et appareils idéologiques d'état" ("Ideology and Ideological State Apparatuses"), Louis Althusser argued that a state transforms individuals into subjects by interpellating (hailing) them in social situations.

BBC. Giving the floor to the public would allow them to make literary 'community programs.' Anyone at all could give the writer an idea, and above all, the precise format for it. The author-public dichotomy would disappear. There'd no longer be the censor on one side, the writer on the other. Just one person: the public-writer as the author."

"That would be a Copernican revolution—or non-revolution. 'Open Door' would at least make people aware how difficult it is to write a good book."[53]

"And more: it would improve the relationship between the writer and his readers. The recipe would create a feeling of participation, a two-way flow. Instead of being a simple receiver of ideas, of values, Mr. Everyman would be a creator. It's a great idea. Worthy of GIAM-BATISTA. But every precaution has to be taken to keep anyone from stealing it."

"Shall we start tomorrow?"

"'Tomorrow' is a word I don't allow in my vocabulary. I've made a pact with the present."

"Take out a patent, perhaps?"

"That would hold up the project's execution."

---

53. Identified in English in Ngal's French text, this literary initiative parodies the Open Door policy promulgated by the United States to support free trade with China and to uphold its territorial integrity against foreign occupation.

"Right away, then!"

"For sure!"

"Tell me, Monsieur, do you know me?"

"No, not at all!"

"Really?"

"I'm afraid you aren't making any sense, Monsieur!"

"Madame, do you recognize GIAMBATISTA?"

"What's that, an animal?"

"No, it's a man."

"Oh, I'm really sorry, Monsieur!"

"Mademoiselle! Mademoiselle!"

"Excuse me, Monsieur, I'm in a hurry."

Perhaps she doubts my good intentions!

"*Chérie*, it's very surprising, it's a real *scandale*. Nobody on the street seems to know GIAMBATISTA!"

"Maybe these are foreigners!"

"No, it's a scandal! Who doesn't know me in this country? I see that we need to write up some interviews ourselves and send them around to all the journals."

"You know well, *chéri*, that I don't approve of such a procedure. That dishonors us!"

"The honor you have in mind is very traditional. Outmoded. *Petit bourgeois*. Some latent conservatism. Conformism. Conventional morality. *Idées reçues*. Done

74

for. What's honor got to do with it, when it's a question of securing my reputation? It's well established in the international world; only a few sons of bitches in this country don't know me. It's intolerable. Illiteracy. Underdevelopment—or, better, being intellectually underequipped. Incurable ills."

"Let's get back to our experiment, *chéri*! I beg you. It should be fruitful."

"It's necessary to find other registers. More accessible to their capacity. It's also possible that my vocabulary is a bit rebarbative. A professional deformation that I can easily remedy."

"Monsieur, Professor Giambatista is in the process of developing a new style, designed to revolutionize the experience of *écriture*. A type of 'Open Door.' Would you be willing to participate in this democratic revolution? It really is a democratic revolution. Up till now, writing has been a bourgeois enterprise that consists of putting totally settled, established ideas into a book. A system of values that you sustain, that you passively receive without taking any part in its creation. 'Open Door' is going to change all that. Democratize writing. You'll be the one who's writing the book yourself. It will no longer be a bourgeois expression but your own work. The end of alienating, bourgeois creation!"

"I completely agree, Monsieur!"

"All the same, some precautions, Monsieur! 'Open Door' admits all ideas, except conservative ones, socially constructed ones . . . you understand!"

"Certainly!"

"Let's get started!"

"The world has gotten to the point that madmen stop people in the street with impunity. They question them. They . . ."

"Hang on. 'Madmen'! You're making fun of me, Monsieur!"

I try the experiment with another passerby.

"Finally, it's the big day. This reminds me of a song we used to squawk out when we were still kids in shorts. It's going to be a beautiful day. It's very hot, and I look forward to finding myself in the freshness of nature, taking off my clothes to get a little sun . . ."

"Thank you, Monsieur, but this seems like some lesson learned by heart. What's more, it lacks consistency and doesn't get us far at all. Goodbye, Monsieur!"

Let's try with a third one.

"I really love discovering places to wander in, picturesque corners of a town. I've already been to this neighborhood, but I've never taken the opportunity to stroll slowly through the streets, for the simple pleasure of discovering it. Today I've got plenty of time, so I want to make use of it. But the joy of finally discovering this town doesn't keep me from casting some admiring glances at a bevy of beautiful women I pass in the street. I'm truly conquered by this town's charm. You don't feel unduly out of place, since the town has a little cosmopolitan corner, which bears quite a resemblance to Montreal. Actually, I know well that Sherbrooke is much more like Montreal than Quebec City, which is a very special town, above all a very French town.[54] Here, there are a lot of English."

"I think this beginning is very nice, Monsieur, like a frame for a novel!"

"Indeed, I could make a frame tale out of it for a novel set in Quebec."

A fourth:

"It's nearly four o'clock when I finally decide to leave my fluffy, cozy bed. I head to the bathroom to make my ablutions, and then I delve into the refrigerator to make myself a generous meal. I'm as hungry as a wolf. My exercises have strengthened my appetite, plus there's the fresh and healthy country air. I cook myself a big marbled steak, well done, with fine baked potatoes. A veritable feast, which I slowly savor while drinking a couple of good bottles of beer. The rest of the day and the evening pass very quietly; I relax on my veranda, listening to the sounds of

---

54. Sherbrooke is the small city in southern Quebec where Ngal began writing his novel.

nature and looking at the starry sky. There are an awful lot of stars to be seen up there. It's been quite a while since I've had the chance to spend an evening gazing at the sky. It's an activity that has its charm, every now and then."

"Hang in there, Monsieur."

"It's not with little tidbits like this that you'll succeed in revolutionizing the experience of writing. Maybe a nonrevolution!"

"The experiment seems inconclusive. Though the masses are indispensable for effecting political revolutions, they seem rather unsuited for literary revolutions. Source of inertia. If they're going to budge, the inspiration has to be breathed into them from elsewhere."

There is one word that I don't dare to pronounce, that can't come out of my mouth. Forbidden. Taboo. Dishonor. Indignity. My genius can't bear to imagine this word, to brush up against it, to toy with it. I hate it.

Traitor, you can't be featured in dictionaries. Forever banned from *francophonie*,[55] from the Republic of Letters. Cursed be the mouth that utters you. Cursed be the mind that imagines you. Cursed be the ears that listen to what's said by a mouth that's cursed itself. Cursed be the nostrils that sniff you. My hatred devours you. Treacherously I pick you out of my teeth. Forever!

---

55. The French-speaking world.

V

Sitting down, leaning on my table. Memories are swarming in my head. Montreal, Saint-Laurent.[56] Wonder of nature. Capricious. Land of men. A mappemonde-globe crowned with suns. Confluence of all races, ruthlessness toward one. Frailty isn't strength. Abandoned to the incommunicability of beings separated by the walls of money, justified by pseudo-scientific myths.

My spirit abolishes space. Bestrides oceans. Sails in the heights. Here I am in Paris, hazy *patrie*.[57] A packed room; a conference. Icarus is flying high. Here I am in Moscow. In Tokyo. In New York. In Nice, the Côte d'Azur. Just my luck to have bad luck. Sunburn. The sun is laughing behind the clouds.

Where am I? In my study. Books scattered around. Some drafts. Symbol of my scattered spirit. Usually I'm quick at finding the most unexpected solutions, but today I feel that all of nature has abandoned me to mourning. Failure . . . The cursed word almost came to my lips. The impotence of a genius is nature's mourning. Night on the horizon, symbol of death. A phrase sprung from

---

56. A district on the outskirts of Montreal noted for its immigrant population.
57. Fatherland.

the echoing depths hovers in my head on a plainchant tune: "When the poet dies, the whole world . . ."[58] My eyes are bulging. It seems as though the whole world is humming this tune. Complicit, my hens have all gone back into their coop. I close the curtains. Here I am, completely shut in. Within four walls upholstered with books. On the table, portraits of the whole family. My radiant wife. Two eyes shining like suns. Lyrical mouth. Black poetry. Nature's *chef-d'œuvre*. A work of genius. Artistic triumph. My eyes dart around and find themselves face-to-face with the portrait of Lautréamont perched indolently atop the cabinet-bookcase.[59] God of writing. At the moment, mute. Is he complicit too? No. Between geniuses, only condolences are allowed. The echo grows on me again, like mustard in my nose. Basically it seems to be conveyed by a contralto voice that makes the whole piece lugubrious. "When the poet dies, the whole world cries."

Knock . . . knock . . . knock . . .

"Yeeesss?"

---

58. A quotation from the 1963 song "Quand il est mort, le poète," by the popular French singer Gilbert Bécaud, on the death of the writer and filmmaker Jean Cocteau.

59. Isidore Ducasse (1846–70), the self-styled Comte de Lautréamont, was a dissolute Uruguayan French poet beloved of the surrealists. He filled his poems with quotations from other writers and argued that all poetry is plagiarism.

"Good day, *Maître!*"

"Ah, it's you! You scared me, Niaiseux! What's the good news?"

"It's bad, actually."

"What is it?"

"It's coming across on teletype machines all around the world, relayed in chorus by every press agency and radio station: 'Unilateral denunciation of every agreement for Afro-Euro-humanitarian cooperation.' Our national radio is pumping this out right now, with unheard-of violence! A brilliant stroke! New stage in the nation's independence!"

"And what about the Associates?"

"General consternation! Black night!"

"There's nothing for me to do but resign."

"Me too. I'm following you."

"I wouldn't want to share the Institute's agony. To participate before history's eyes in the incapacity of the Africanolators to govern themselves; their incapacity for scientific research."

"It's time for us to leave. Do you know what the other camp is whispering in these dark hours? 'You're afraid to take up your duties.' Mademoiselle Castino Paqua is preparing your courses. She'll write you a short note; she'll give you some breathing room. If she leaves, it'll mean your slow eclipse until you finally die.

And more: they say your essays are the worst kind of hoax. Displays of fake wisdom from a deceptive erudition. Plagiarism. Mere chattering. Commonplaces. Based on what? Uncited book reviews from *Culture et développement*.[60]

"And who's the real author of your poetry? Mademoiselle Castino Paqua, with here and there phrases lifted from all the great poets. Disguised translations from Latin, presented as originals. The Roman poets pillaged. Catullus is the one most damaged by your frauds.

"And there's more. Sartre, Althusser, the true heirs of Marx and Lenin, are going to be seized upon. Your crimes have to be denounced. Several publishers have already been contacted, to work out a common line to follow. The affair's tentacles are spreading in every direction. Everyone claims to have been injured. Public opinion is up in arms over your violations. On the street it's said you let yourself be associated with criminal enterprises. Your '*Open Door*' is supposed to be a cleverly organized mechanism for what's called 'the most abominable moral fraud of the century.' Thanks to it, amateurs were going to have written a novel two or three hundred

---

60. Echoing the name of the Belgian social science journal *Cultures et développement*.

pages long, and you were going to put your signature on it. What was presented in a democratic guise was really nothing other than a deception of public opinion.

"Such initiatives are disturbing on the political level. Equated to the alienation of the people. They plan to accuse you of skillfully maneuvering to enslave the common people. All your books as advocating subversion. What is this war that you wage against *idées reçues*, against everything settled? You openly want to throw over traditional morality in order to substitute your own, hidden under pompous appellations like 'progressive ideas,' 'ethics of sincerity,' 'ethics of liberty.'

"And even more. The most serious accusation is of inciting people to alienating practices. The origin of this accusation seems to be your liaison with Mademoiselle Castino Paqua, whose erotic—in fact, unnatural— theories are well known. Certain statements in particular, taken from the interrogation of your *amie*, have been introduced as evidence:

> 'Eroticism can assist in the discovery of a new
> world.'
> 'And more than that: it's progress.'
> 'The erotic man will be a new animal.'
> 'The taboos of bourgeois morality are economic in
> origin.'

'The new law, the good law, proclaims that it is
        right and good to make love well, and
        to do it freely.'
'Virginity isn't a virtue.'
'The couple is a limitation, marriage a prison.'
'Couples should be outlawed. A third person
        should be added to the couple.'
'You need to constantly offer yourself, give
        yourself, keep uniting your body to more
        bodies, and to count as wasted the hours
        spent outside their arms.'[61]

Those are some samples. Apparently they've amassed more than five hundred propositions. Their accusation emphasizes the alienating aspect of the practices to which this insolent doctrine leads in Africa.

"And still more. They've discovered your *amie* in the process of converting Africans; there is supporting evidence. She personally makes a spectacle of herself. What kind of spectacle? Unnatural. On her own or with someone else. You've been associated with all these acrobatic exercises yourself. You practice that kind of wrestling hold.

"And still more. The contempt you've displayed for Blacks. Your anti-Africanization of the Institute. Your

---

61. All of these quotations are taken from the novel *Emmanuelle*.

inciting of certain Nationals and Associates to revolt against the decisions of their superiors.

"All these grievances are being peddled from mouth to mouth and keep growing, fed as if by the ocean's swells, by what's called the radio of the street. Commented on, amplified."

"My dear Niaiseux, the dog barks, the caravan passes by. My genius won't put up any longer with the Black rabble. What do they have in common with me? And as for us? Right now, we're shut up in this study. We understand one another, have the same experience of them. It's as if you were crossing an abyss. The crowd—stupid by nature because it's irrational—is incapable of joining the most revolutionary project ever conceived. Under other skies, today I'd be in the news. But here I am, reduced to nothingness."

"You usually lead the way for the country. Now, everything's black night. Yet you always manage to play the victim, to turn things in your favor. Public opinion is easily maneuvered; it's the name of the game. The ball is now in your court. Today, opinion will respond to what you ask of it. The 'Open Door' that you're looking for? They'll serve it up to you. It looks like your enemies are in the streets, in the houses, behind every door, but they're composing a scenario that your own genius could never manage to match. You want to give the crowd, the masses, a great responsibility. The irony of fate wants them to have it. Your genius seeks to create a true feeling of participation, of a two-way current. The people understand you. You're democratizing the structures of communication, you're revolutionizing them; you're making them into a vehicle for values, bringing opinion your way. You've succeeded, never more than in these painful hours. You've succeeded despite yourself in bridging the chasm that separates the indefinite crowd from yourself, the writer. You want to get the writer out of his solitude, and the crowd is dragging you into the public square. This novel that you want to associate with them, you'll be the one to write. With letters of gold. Under the skies where they'll lead you. Here, the 'radio of the street' has as much importance as the public ministry that's accusing you. That's what guards the security of the State, detects enemies, decides their fate. It's all-powerful. An anonymous force. An infernal machine. Uncontrollable. Implacable. Even before anyone has determined whether an accusation is well founded, it has already acted. Has struck. Its verdict is often irreparable.

"As for your friends? Don't count on them. As soon as they smell smoke, they disappear. Everybody takes care of themselves. That includes the Associates, who have lost everything in this country. Self-interest: in the end, that's what links people. For them you were all-powerful,

Providence, Father. Today you're a dirty Black among the Blacks. Blackly black. Oh, no! You aren't a Black, you're way above that. Your star doesn't have any black in it. It glows even when it's extinguished."

"Woes come so that people can understand themselves. Not to arouse pity; that doesn't exist. For us to reveal to ourselves the relation between one existence and another, the abyss that separates beings, their opacity."

The knell has sounded. What remains of genius? The force of the soul. Even once it has lost everything. To bequeath courage to posterity in the face of the present makes an imperishable book. History is full of examples. The greatest French geniuses are perhaps not those who are called writers in the usual sense of the term, but those who have distinguished the homeland of Joan of Arc, of Napoleon, by their grandeur of spirit. Courage makes us immortal.

PART TWO

VI

Here we are, outside human time. Here we are; here we'll stay. The room is barely two meters by three, by four high. Just enough to keep from suffocating. The walls smooth. Not a single window. Completely shut in.

"If I understand correctly, we're already in eternity before the fact?"

"A temporal immobility!"

"Yes, and without a watch! The days and nights are just alike."

"It's the realization of your dream!"

"Hardly in the circumstances I would have wished for."

"I'm worried about the fate that's being planned for you, *Maître*. We could be in this dungeon for four or five months, or this could last many years. But I expect several months anyway."

"Provided that a verdict is rendered."

"I suppose an interrogation will precede the verdict. That isn't always the case, it seems! Sometimes, people are released without a verdict. It's judged that you've been punished enough for what you've been accused of."

"But in our case, who is the accuser? Public opinion? What are we being accused of?"

"The jailor could be our go-between and tell us."

"If we're lucky enough to encounter one. It isn't even certain that he'd know the charges against us."

"However things work out, *Maître*, my greatest happiness is to have been so closely associated with your fate. It isn't given to everyone to experience the final moments of a genius. It's the most beautiful book one could ever read!"

"In short, Niaiseux, my life itself is a book! Posterity will render—and already renders me—the testimony I deserve."

"In the evening of their life, great men have always confided their last thoughts. Think of Socrates. If Plato hadn't been present, we'd never have known anything of his doctrine or his teachings. Fate has put us here side by side. During the coming days and months, we'll be breathing the same air, experiencing the same anxieties, the same anguish. If by any chance I survive you, I'll be the sole witness able to describe your final moments. Your luminous thought at the ultimate moment will be collected by the one who all his life has devoted to you a cult unto death."

"Dear friend, one thing is certain: I don't renounce anything of my credo. I'm not a Lévy-Bruhl who went back on his own principles at the end of his life.[62] I won't warm myself with any such bonfire. By the force of events we find ourselves closed up here as if in a womb. Primordial space. My dream. Receptacle. Cavern. Vase. Wineskin. We've been installed here now not by any desire arising from our own volition but by a masculine aggressivity. I don't regret this. We are placed in a metaphor that responds well to what would have been my life's dream. Gentle irony that holds the genius and frees him from contingencies. One enters this hole armed with letters made golden by courage.

"You've never been such a good lecturer as today. What you say sinks into me. They seek to make us atrophy! Render us impotent! But our intellectual virility is greater than ever. Our lucidity keener than ever. We're being reduced to the state of seeking to be loved more than to love. We're being rejected. This is what this hole, this cavity, this void symbolizes. Nonetheless, a void of plenitude. I possess myself. I am no longer theirs. They have taken time away from us. They refuse us the past

---

62. In posthumously published notebooks, *Les carnets* (1949), the French ethnographer Lucien Lévy-Bruhl contemplated abandoning the theory of pre-logical thought that he advanced in works such as *La mentalité primitive* (*The Primitive Mind*, 1922).

and the future. They are condemning us to the present. You can't say 'yesterday,' 'today,' 'tomorrow.' Even the Inuit at the North Pole have a right to an Indian summer, but this is denied us. The present! Eternal present, I adore you! I invoke you, I love you. You are here. Your uninterrupted presence is the only companion given to me. I am filled up with you."

"*Maître*, you've traveled extensively, gotten to know people. What is your most profound thought about humanity?"

"It seems to me that man's essence is like a scent. Wherever you go, you smell it, you smell it! But you can never really inhale it. You sense the scent, but the substance remains invisible to you, ungraspable. A man is like a perfume to his fellow. Precious, if it leads to the establishment of a *détente* between them. Noxious, if it instills a state of tension. That is why man is never at rest. He never gives himself to others except by the law of self-interest, which clothes itself in multiple forms: love, money, servitude. Indifference itself is an expression of concealed self-interest. Malraux, in a flash of insight, says: 'What is man? A bunch of little secrets.'[63] For myself, I'd say: a bunch of little self-interests."

---

63. In his novel *Les noyers de l'Altenburg* (*The Walnut Trees of Altenburg*), André Malraux wrote, "Pour l'essentiel, l'homme est ce qu'il cache. . . .

"Two geniuses, two definitions!"

"If you like! You love reconciliations, just so! 'A bunch of little self-interests' wrapped up in a dense opacity. That's what weighs down the human condition. You can read it in every face. On the lips of the salesgirl who smiles to attract you to her merchandise; in the eyes of the woman you love, with whom you'd like to fuse yourself but who remains separated from you by the space that divides you from her. That is why my life is a continual combat against space. To escape space. Destroy it. The vocation of every true philosophy. My system aims for nothing other than that. Connect these 'bunches of self-interest' by a linkage that transcends space. I want to see writing—my true religion—as this place of transcendence. All my research seeks to establish this new science of *écriture*. Gestural writing, womb of freedom and initiative, for the writer and equally for the reader. Plenitude of sense. Flux and reflux of subterranean thought. Finally, the writer can emerge from his solitude. The reader can be restored to his true personality; delivered from passivity. Writing finally secularized, so to say, rendered democratic. For the laity—the Greek *laos*: the people. The public becomes coauthor with the writer, the

---

Un misérable petit tas de secrets" ("Fundamentally, man is what he hides. . . . A wretched little pile of secrets"; 54; 67).

abyss that separates them finally bridged. Space-abyss! Horrible! The world is reconciled, antagonisms faded away. What a revolution!

"Like *le poète maudit*, I'm misunderstood. Misrecognized. Despised. Rejected. Banished, like a brigand. I only want to serve the people, humanity. Here I am, dragged through the mud. Worse than a criminal. Once they're aware of this injustice, the Writers' Union will protest. The philistines, to their confusion, will release me. But look how I'm projecting myself into the future. What a crazy, deadly hope. The present, where are you? Come back, come back! No, you're always here, my friend!"

A key turns in the lock. The door opens. A beam of light invades the entire room. Violation of our solitude!

"Foreigners' lapdogs, it seems that you want to overthrow the regime, preaching revolution out on the street!"

My eyes are no longer accustomed to the light; my ears have trouble bearing the outburst of the guard's thundering voice. The door shuts.

A blow lands straight on Niaiseux's neck. "You, piece of foreign crap, how dare you support and incite this misguided man who's so full of himself?"

Niaiseux falls headfirst. His chin smashes against the floor. He groans. When he gets up, two of his teeth are

94

lying there, white as crystals, disrupting the blackness of the room. The man tells him to pick them up.

"Swallow them, dog!" he orders.

Niaiseux picks them up. He does as he's told. The man attacks.

One doesn't affront the ancestral order with impunity. When a white man violates it, that's understandable! It's in his nature to defy nature. When a countryman becomes his accomplice, the ancestors' anger will consume him.

Looking fixedly at me, the guard spits on the ground. Sign of supreme contempt. A shiver of indignation runs through my head. The faint echo of a certain voice goes through me. The man's eyes don't leave me. He seems to have been sent by someone, but who? And why? He turns threatening. The whole room is filled with noise. A blow of unheard-of violence aimed at my head throws me against a wall. The entire dungeon seems to be traversed by points of light. Shooting stars go out from the center to bombard the periphery. A second blow knocks me to the floor. I get back up. I don't make a single cry. A line of poetry comes to mind: "It's just as cowardly to cry, to groan, to pray."[64] I hold myself back. The monster

---

64. From Alfred de Vigny's 1843 philosophical poem "La mort du loup" ("Death of the Wolf"; Œuvres 102; 100–02), which envisions a dying wolf telling his hunter to accept fate without complaining.

is still in the room. In a corner. Enraged. The only force his two prey have to oppose him is our weakness. Unequal combat. Lambs to the slaughter.

"Do not suppose, filthy curs, that we will fall into the trap of making martyrs out of traitors. Martyrs of what? The one, of your inanity. The other, of your pride. Exploiting your own people to serve the foreigners! Daring to address yourselves to the ancestors, not sparing any traditional ceremony, in order to equal the Whites. Calling our ceremonies savage rites and then exploiting them for commercial purposes! Trampling on all our ancestral wisdom! Treating it as fetishism! Unpardonable crimes! Listen well! The child who disowns its mother has no right to any looks of pity. We have been affronted day and night. Day by day, we have followed all your conversations with your so-called Associates.

"Dirty monster, we have suffered the contempt you have displayed toward us, toward the entire human race. Great writer, have you forgotten the sessions of initiation? You took no notice of the forewarnings, the premonitions. Only savage ceremonies, no doubt! You have disturbed our sleep and that of our dead; insulted our gods—sacrilege!

"Your research on space—was that just so you can live only with Whites? The Blacks don't have a place! You've excluded them from the human race. What an injury you've done them. They are peaceful. They've given you everything—even the possibility of rejecting them. Maybe you should have gone to a clinic, a blood bank, to get a transfusion, draining out your blood to replace it with white blood! Press the logic to its conclusion. A journey to the end of the night, à la Céline?[65] One prick of the needle, and in the blink of an eye you're White! As for the other attributes of Blackness, a little plastic surgery could get rid of the remaining imperfections— the flatness of your nose, the thickness of your lips, the color of your eyes, the frizziness of your hair! You cannot see any possibility for human beings to develop except through 'whitening.' Otherwise, no salvation. Regression. Animality. Antinatural. Anticultural. Archaism. Prehistory. Primitive mentality. Realm of myths. Fatalities. Constraints.

"Press your logic farther. You exist within history; as for us, we're outside of history. Perhaps above history. You have recourse to us in order to 'take off.' Have you asked yourself about the very possibility of communication between such 'different' stages of humanity? So far

---

65. In Louis-Ferdinand Céline's 1932 novel *Voyage au bout de la nuit* (*Journey to the End of the Night*), the antihero Bardamu wanders through the battlefields of World War I, the jungles of colonial Africa, and industrial Detroit before finally settling in Paris as a doctor to the poor.

'distant' by so many millions of light years? The abyss between your discourse and ours is uncrossable. Our discourse is nourished on myths, on legends. Our logic supports itself with proverbs. What platform for dialogue could you set up between yourself and us? Your discourse is a tissue of references to foreign philosophers, to modes of thought elaborated through every excess, the worst subversions, and the loosening of morals. Your alienation does not lie in the fact of having left us, but in the attempted reforestation of your identity. A Europe stripped bare seeks to replant entire regions, to give itself the illusion of having forests. Its history has become an endless nostalgia for what it has lost. But have there ever been lost paradises? The West, at any rate, maintains this illusion through an abundant literature. As for you, you're leaving us. You break every psychological link with us. You artificially suppress the natural within yourself. Then, in order to liberate yourself, you dare to address yourself to us once again? Do you see the contradiction? Have you forgotten all those European saints who could come to your aid? Jean-Jacques Rousseau. Bernardin de Saint Pierre.[66] Chateaubriand, with whom your infatu-

---

66. Bernardin de Saint Pierre is best known for his 1788 novel *Paul et Virginie*, set on the island of Mauritius in the Indian Ocean. The novel contrasts life in a pure state of nature with the corruption of French society, in terms echoing Jean-Jacques Rousseau's 1755 *Discours sur*

ated head is filled. Not just proponents but heroes of en-slavement! You genius, identify yourself heroically with them! You'll turn back into the rustling of trees!"

The man opens the door. Slams it behind him. Throughout his discourse, my legs seemed paralyzed. The pain from the heavy blow of his fist was in abeyance; now I feel it again. Niaiseux is lying down. Is he really sleeping? I don't dare to wake him. Why disturb him? My head is aching so badly that I can't concentrate at all. I am seized with anguish. No doubt some vengeance is being readied. But what kind? In what forms? Physical tortures? Humiliations? Or both? How long will we be dwelling here? Is this only a test? An initiation?

"The pedagogy of suffering begins. I sense the most absolute void within myself. Any interior voyage, absurd! No end. No depth. For the first time, life seems to me the inverse of the plenitude that has always defined me. Violence watches over us. Violence surrounds us on all sides. Malevolent. Menacing. Instinctual. Mythic . . . Rit-ual. Nourishing. The people feed themselves on it. Here we are, sacrificial victims. Bitter metaphor! Yes, a met-aphor! Culture is dying in me so that it can be reborn. I make myself the ground zero on which it can set its

---

l'origine et les fondements de l'inégalité parmi les hommes (Discourse on the Origin and Basis of Inequality among Men).

foundations. Oh, sacred violence,[67] here I am, ready, like a Socrates! You, at least you are the only one who understands me. I desire this *rendez-vous* inscribed in destiny. I adore you. I prostitute myself for you. All culture comes from you: language, the imaginary, societies. You are the mother of all. You govern everything. You are the true queen. The true repressed. You will immolate me. Here I am, chosen victim. The true *savoir*. The true initiation. No other sacrificial explanation. You are self-sufficient. Man is born from you. Human truth is your daughter. Primordial order where everything meets. From which everything takes root."

"*Maître*, I'm not asleep. The pain is so intense, I feel like my jaw is going to fall off. I hear you. Your words are soothing. Your thought has never attained such depth. I've always heard of violence as a parasite. But now for the first time, it appears to me in a Lacanian light.[68] It's necessary for you to be at the evening of your life for humanity to benefit from this exceptional grace."

---

67. Viko here echoes the ideas of the critic and anthropologist René Girard. In his 1972 work *La violence et le sacré* (*Violence and the Sacred*), Girard proposed that culture is based on primal acts of ritual violence and that Christianity uniquely advocates self-sacrifice rather than the sacrifice of others.

68. The psychoanalyst Jacques Lacan (1901–81) argued for the transformative power of a violent rupture of one's thoughts and identity.

"Not my life's evening but its springtime! I consider these supreme moments as the renaissance of my life, of culture. What is true arises from nature. Nature springing out of itself, doubling itself. It is like the rapport of the real with the imaginary.[69] It is violence that accomplishes this first leap. Culture is carried by a constant violence. It engenders itself in violence. It nourishes all the socioeconomic and political mutations of violence."

"Doesn't such a theory conceal ambiguity?'

"As do all profound intuitions! It isn't a question of appealing to violence, nor to totalitarianism. But of a sacralization of the womb, as the possibility for human nature to accomplish its own self-transcendence. Of course, 'nature' in the historical sense of the term. This is no place to be thinking of the desiccated concept of the Thomist Scholastics.[70] I consider that you, who have the signal opportunity to share these unique moments—if your suffering doesn't carry you away along with me— you will be the universal heir of my thought. If only you don't distort it!"

---

69. In Lacan's theory, developed in his *Écrits* and elsewhere, *the real* is the natural state from which we are cut off by language; *the imaginary* is a fantasy that is meant to compensate for the self's fundamental state of lack and the self's loss of the real.

70. Medieval Neoplatonist academics, followers of Thomas Aquinas.

"What a heavy responsibility! It would take your genius to keep it safe from intellectual embezzlement by your enemies."

"That doesn't matter. The essential thing is that humanity keep the spark of truth that's offered to it. You are the channel. If you're carried off at the same time as I am, the poor human race will miss a chance that may never come again."

"Hush! Someone's coming!"

The door opens. In comes a man built like an orangutan. Niaiseux stands up. I make a sign to him to keep his *sang-froid*.[71] Our last moment, I'd say! A single blow will suffice to bump us off. The man's face is masked. Could there be some connection to the vision I had at night in my study? Two sharply pointed teeth adorn the corners of his mouth. Is he a hit man, sent to case out the scene? What kind of death are they planning for us? Strangulation? Hanging? A simple pistol shot? The man doesn't have anything with him. He doesn't need to be armed. Would he even know how to handle a gun if someone gave him one? He seems to be located on the border between human and animal.

He looks fixedly at each of us in turn. A quizzical and somewhat stupidly baffled look. As if to say: this isn't

---

71. "Composure."

worth the bother. What is he looking for? We are pet-rified with fright. If only he'd get it over with, I say to myself. After a moment he takes a deep breath. An acrid odor fills the room. If he stays very long, I think, he'll use up the little oxygen that remains for us. Then, a look of utter disdain. He goes back out, closing the door without saying a word.

"Are we going to have a revival here of the theater piece in my study? With the difference that I'm no longer the master of ceremonies? Am I really a prisoner, or am I still the maestro of the orchestra as always? Those people have the illusion that I'm in their control. But in fact, I'm the one controlling them! They're going to line up for the *danse macabre*.[72] I make them dance. Their emotions, their resentments, their unleashed instincts are what animate the orgy that awaits us, but I am the inspiration for it. Without me, none of this would have taken place. I'll have been fortunate for humanity up to the very last moment."

"It's enigmatic, the attitude of this species, homo sapi-ens! I'd thought that from one moment to the next we'd become nothing more than a bundle of souvenirs for humanity!"

---

72. The *danse macabre* (dance of death) was a medieval allegory in which skeletons escorted humans to their graves; that allegory is the subject of *Danse macabre* (1874), a famous tone poem by Camille Saint-Saëns.

"In an individual like that, there aren't two languages. Only one: physical force. Nature has endowed him with brute wealth. It is primal material that needs to be transformed. He lives in this primary stage, characterized by the lack of any cultural doubling. *Speculum de l'autre homme.*"[73]

"How will he advance to it?"

"With such individuals, the self-creative power is so weak, or so weakened by the social environment, that they need to be inspired from beyond themselves. I don't deny the humanity within him, but it's submerged, held down by the heavy dictates of animality."

"But would he be able to open himself to such an exterior inspiration?"

"It will be a matter of getting him out of his intimacy with nature—in short, to make him a traitor to the secret that joins him simply to the earth, to the stars, to the plants, to the animals, and to make him celebrate the quotidian mixed with rationality. Not the disenchanted rationality that's developed in the West, but the kind of rationality in which reason and nature each play their part. Supreme wisdom!"

---

73. "Speculum of the other man"—playing on *Speculum de l'autre femme* (*Speculum of the Other Woman*), by the Lacanian feminist Luce Irigaray, who criticized the phallocentrism of Western philosophy and psychology from Aristotle to Freud.

"In sum, an infusion of rationality in nature!"

"Just so. It's a matter of the dosage. Neither hypermysticism nor hyperrationality. Either denatures the human being."

"Who would be able to carry out such an operation?"

"It has less to do with a body of knowledge given from outside than with the insertion of Africa's supposed 'ethnographic present'—a term I don't much love[74]—in the present moment of our historical development, in the dialectic of mythic determinisms and of liberty. Our insertion in this dialectic is already an accomplished fact, but it's necessary to accelerate the process. What is holding it back is a so-called cultural revolution that jumbles together and props up old habitudes, old customs, old ideas that were certainly justifiable in the mythic universe but that are not consistent with the modern world. The past cannot be denied. It exists within us; but it should only be taken into consideration in relation to the present. Yet this doesn't depend on a purely political decision. Many African customs don't hold up against the combined shock of the present and the future. There

---

74. Viko shares this dislike with the anthropologist Johannes Fabian, who taught at the University of Zaire in 1973; in *Time and the Other* (1983), Fabian criticized ethnographers who present primitive cultures by writing in an "ethnographic present" outside the flow of history (80).

ought to be a spontaneous selection. That is how a certain form of rationality will ensconce itself, whether anyone likes it or not. The dialectic of the success or lack of success—or the outright failure—of maintaining this or that degrading custom at any cost. It will produce what one could call 'an epistemological power failure' that will make Africans see the real in a new light, make them treat time and space—those keywords—in a prospective fashion. A subterranean labor, patient, like that of the mole."

VII

A pause. Niaiseux suffers terribly in silence. Philosophically. As for me, once I stop talking, I feel as though my
skull will burst. Not a sigh. Not a single groan.

The lock grates again. The door opens. A man enters,
dressed in a goat skin, biceps ringed with silver bracelets.
Head covered with a headdress all in pearls, crowned
with parrot feathers. He is followed by a handsome
young man in an elegant suit. The door closes behind
them. Even though the door is closed, this time the room
remains bright; the source of light is invisible.

In a flash of insight, I perceive the reason for our confinement. My indiscretions in my study are now having
their effect. But I don't breathe a word to Niaiseux.

The man turns to the youth. Speaks to him at length.
The young man translates in turn:

"Dogs and sons of dogs! My dignity, my honor forbid
me to address you directly. Your crime is immeasurable.
You will pay for it with the last drop of your blood. But
do not dream of being thought of as martyrs; you will
not have that honor. The fundamental reason that keeps
me from addressing you directly is that our universes—
speech and writing—have nothing in common. You
have impiously set an abyss between yourselves and us.

You have chosen the universe of the book—the space of inscription—abandoning that which nourished your childhood, fed your dreams, and furnished your subconscious. You have tried to drain away this lake of symbols, images, the core that welds together our community's cultural cohesion. We are total strangers to you.

"We have followed your alienation with heavy hearts. But we knew that you would never go too far, that a nostalgia would bring you back to our shores. Disdainfully rejected, the sacred riches of orality always leave the guilty ones with an odor that pursues them like a gnawing remorse. The gravity of your impiety resides in your attempt to desacralize orality. You have wanted to appropriate the freedom, the space, the time of the storyteller; to introduce them into novelistic discourse. An atheist's attempt, destitute of faith! Not even stopping at this degree of criminality, you have had the presumption to become initiated into our rites, hoping thus to arrive at your goal. In so doing, you would subvert orality and Western discourse alike. You would give birth to hybrid characters, heroes, texts! That is why this sacrilege cannot go unpunished.

"But first, you will be given a truth potion that will cause you to confess all your other crimes against humanity. You will have to disavow all the misdeeds you have perpetrated at the Institute. The Blacks at the Institute are human beings just as much as the Associates. You do not consider them human beings. It is neither the skin nor the erudition that gives a man his value, but that which has escaped you even to the present. I have spoken."

This so persuasive discourse vanquishes me by the strength of its evidence. For the first time, the opposition orality/writing appears to me in a completely unexpected light. If orality imposes the law of the sacred, writing does the same for the profane. Written language isn't a variation of oral language: they are two universes, each with a history lost in the depths of time. Opposed trajectories. Two types of humanity, and yet . . . not irreconcilable!

The young man shows evidence of elevated culture. Is his discourse—of a blinding and instructive clarity—a translation, or is it a tendentiously embroidered commentary of his own? I ask myself! Then our fate is sealed. Several minutes of silence . . . We'll have to pay for my impiety. In a flash, Michelet saw France and his soul together.[75] I, Giambatista, see my soul vanishing, *"my way*

75. In the preface to his 1869 *Histoire de France*, Jules Michelet wrote that his massive project was conceived in a flash of insight when he perceived France "comme une âme et une personne" ("as a soul and a person"; 1: 45). Appropriately, Michelet was strongly influenced by Vico, whose *Scienza nuova* he translated into French.

of life" dissolving, like sulfur in water. Africa, you are the conqueror! No, you aren't yet! You haven't got the last word. Nonetheless, you've had the first one: in effect, the road to rebirth comes with the rekindling of faith in oneself.

The man makes a sign to the young man, inviting him to leave the room. After a moment, he returns with a pitcher. A new sign is given. The young man approaches me. With a curt gesture, he invites me to drink it all down. To empty the pitcher in three drafts. It's up to me to make the division, Why three? Africa's profound understanding proceeds through the interpretation of signs and symbols. The African writer merely floats on the surface if he is content only to celebrate the continent in its anguish, its pain, its resentments, its frustration, its repressions, its deep and ardent desires, its joys. Writing has to make itself both sign and symbol, a universe of correspondences. Lightning flash of a ravishing moment that my genius experiences before dying. The words of Goethe come back to me: "Stay a while, moment, you are so lovely."[76] Triumphant past, caress me. Present,

---

76. In Johann Wolfgang von Goethe's *Faust* (1808), when Faust makes his pact with the devil, he agrees that if Mephistopheles gives him anything that pleases him so much that he wants to stay in the moment forever, he will die at that instant (49).

ravish me. Space, expand me. Let me die in all of you. Let me be reborn in you!

Where are they taking me, like a sheep to the slaughter? Will it be to a true initiation, like an intrepid navigator sailing down great rivers and out to sea?

I follow the injunctions. Drumbeats mark the rhythm of the three drafts. Little by little my eyes must become wild to those who look at me. Shapes lose their clarity. A ringing begins in my ears. A concert of grating and discordant voices settles into me.

Hallucination from the real and the imaginary? Yes, wisdom. I see monsters. Toads. Grasshoppers devouring ants. Three sharp blows on my shoulders and spine throw me to my knees. And I start vomiting up slimy frogs. Crabs. Then more than one viscous liquid. Even so, I don't lose my lucidity.

"Stranger, you are now going to confess your crimes against humanity. The truth potion has made this task easy for you. It is no longer possible for you to hide anything at all from us. Your lucidity is a one-way street. That is to say, once you have proffered a true statement, it will no longer be possible for you to go back on it. This is pure immediacy! Our lie detector. Filthy cur of a stranger, you will note well that we have no need of a complicated apparatus shackling the head in a crowd of brain waves. Since there is no danger of the secret being revealed, I can explain it simply to you. The creatures you have seen emerging from your stomach were administered in the truth potion. The crabs have the task of scratching the stomach's walls, to wound certain fibers connected with the nervous system. The pain that follows would ordinarily have been atrocious, had we not also administered the frogs, whose mission was to secrete a soothing liquid that swiftly heals every wound. That is the whole truth in its astonishing simplicity.

"Moreover, we will be able to determine whether your conscience is normal from the kind of faults to which you confess. Now begin."

"I confess that I have involved myself with the base maneuvers of my sinister colleagues Haïna and Malawi to smear an innocent student. What is more, I deeply despise these two colleagues. The first for his incompetence, which is a subject of discussion among his students, more often in the hallways than in the classrooms, and this individual is said to have a dubious, unverifiable diploma. Some of his students are more competent than he is. His methods of analysis are forty years old—if he has any methods at all!

"As for Malawi, his diploma is in order. Like the other, he is fundamentally tribalist. For a decade, the students have had to suffer the nonsense that he embroiders around his maternal language.

"I acknowledge my guilt.

"I confess to hating a *confrère* of international reputation.[77] I can't bear his presence. I was created to be number one everywhere. I've been offended by his merits. With the aid of my juniors, I have organized defamatory actions against him. The Associates were very skillfully informed. The result was achieved. Decrease in sympathy. Empty space around him. And more. I instituted a reign of terror. I imposed an intellectual dictatorship at the heart of the Institute.

"I acknowledge my guilt, my very great guilt.

"The Associates themselves were not spared. To me, they were mere instruments that I utilized, whether to combat the Nationals who had raised their heads a little too high, or to undertake work for my personal ends. The Associates are humans too. They shouldn't be used as instruments. Humanity doesn't have any color.

"I acknowledge my very great guilt.

"Among the Associates, there is one whom I must specially mention. Wanting to screw him over, I invented the most implausible infamies concerning him.

---

77. *Confrère* means "colleague."

"I acknowledge my too, too great guilt.

"I didn't spare anyone. The authorities got theirs too. I have incited my colleagues against them. They went about bowing their heads. My conduct has been based on hypocrisy and perfidy. To me, the heads of the administration are perfect imbeciles, promoted into their positions by sordid interests.

"I acknowledge my very great guilt.

"I hate the human race. I do not know what friendship is. A truce in the relations between two people! A friend is someone who reflects my image. In short, my double.

"My guilt against the human race is inexpiable.

"I acknowledge this unconditionally."

———————

"You total monster! Now we will offer you a little erotic-masochistic pleasure that is allowed to everyone who undergoes the truth potion."

They have the Orangutan come in. They point out Niaiseux, who up until now has had no other role than the pleasure of being a spectator. The active portion of the trial begins. The man charges at him. He knows the job, having done it hundreds of times. He seizes Niaiseux by his hair, lifts him up to his own level, and spits with full force into his face. He lets him fall down again. He picks him up and throws him to the ground without picking him up again. Niaiseux falls back heavily, like a body without a skeleton. For the first time in my life, I am filled with pity. The spectacle tears from me the spontaneous cry: *"This* is what a man is!"[78] My outcry barely attracts any attention from the audience overcome by the cruelty of the scene.

The man is given a huge needle, heated white-hot. He brutally strips Niaiseux. He plunges it through the penis of my poor friend, who gives the most horrible scream ever heard. To prevent a hemorrhage, the executioner puts black powder into the hole left by the needle. He pushes it even farther in, then attaches a ring to its end, from which he suspends a bell with a high-pitched sound, making it audible from far away. Furthermore, the bell enables Niaiseux to avoid encountering anyone of the opposite sex in a cultural sanctuary. The regular jingling of the bell alerts women to hide themselves away when Niaiseux goes by. Symbol of the ignominy inflicted on traitors.

All these developments have repercussions in the other sanctuaries. It is decided to overwhelm me once and for all by confronting me with masters of speech before handing me over to the fate that is reserved for me.

---

78. Viko's exclamation ("C'est ça l'homme!" in French) now replaces Buffon's "Le style, c'est l'homme."

At the trial, each of the premier centers of culture, of initiation, and of occultism will be represented by its chair and a highly qualified cultural counselor. The sanctuary for Komodibi of Nyamina and of Bougouni;[79] the sanctuaries of Bokanana d'Amey; the geomancy centers of Nionsonbougou; the occultist centers of Labé, Dia de Tombouctou, Djenné, Hamdallahix, Bandiagara, and Guirir; those of Bossomnoré, Todjam, Bura-Saba, Yaté, Badinogo, Ramatoulaya, Barami, Duahubou, Mamé, and Sagbtenga; the magic centers of Darsalami "for attainment by the infernal rite of the chicken," of the Airumba of Louroum "to cure the sterility of African firefighters"—which is to say, "wearers of old and ugly pants" from Bélédougou and of the Mandé; the initiatory centers for the Pende and Tshokwe peoples, and so on; in short, the entire continent is represented. Worthily represented.

People are already speaking of the trial of the century. "The continent has been betrayed, attacked; it is necessary to return the challenge." "It's necessary to finish this once and for all." "No continent has been appointed to culturally direct the others." "We consider that it is

---

79. The sanctuaries in Nyamina and Bougouni in Mali, traditionally known for its oral culture, were places where *Komodibi* (bards) would receive training and undergo rites of initiation. Other sites listed are elsewhere in Africa.

culture, properly understood, that creates a people's dignity." "We feel ourselves strong enough today to become exporters of culture." "We're already exporting it." "How can anyone still keep talking to us about 'savagery' after Hitler's cannibalistic displays?" "We don't have any 'subculture.'" "Culture in its own right!" "We refuse to be guinea pigs for Western ethnologists." "We are not prehistoric curiosities!" "We have always had faith in ourselves." "There is no counterculture in Africa." "Counterculture is a Western monstrosity; it has nothing at all to do with us." "If the wheels have come off the West, we are ready to teach it how to rediscover them." "We are not an unnatural society, nor a denatured society, nor a denatured other nature." "These notions will never be allowed to take root in Africa." "The time is over when we could be taken as pure objects for a science that has been universally denounced as the political practice of human alienation." "Western science—especially in its ethnological form—is the translation of the West's incapacity to rejoin the subjectivity of those it abusively labels 'primitives.'" "It is inconceivable that Africa's sons could ever have been guilty of such aberrations!" "The contempt for the continent displayed by this misguided dog is immeasurable." "Is he really normal?" "Shouldn't he be subjected to a treatment to restore his mental equilibrium?"

Thus is a great brouhaha raised by the young men who accompanied the heads of the various sanctuaries. Elegantly dressed, expressing themselves in impeccable French. All of them educated at Western universities, some in Paris, London, Geneva, Brussels, others in America. Are they benevolent cultural technocrats, or have they been coopted in those locations through a fate like mine? A question I could never elucidate. To judge from their remarks, they seem to be as convinced of their African specificity as the *maîtres* they serve. They also seem equally hostile to my cause. Formed within the Western dialectic, they no doubt want to crush me with the weight of their arguments. They've set themselves on solid ground. Their position is unassailable. As for mine, based on quicksand, will it hold up against their assaults? I've never in my life felt so cruelly defeated. My brilliant career in the world of *savants* now seems ridiculous to me. The Club of Rome, to which I belong as of right, falls away. My hypotheses on the reconciliation of the writer with the public, on the renovation of humanity through values other than those perceived by the Club's report, my hypotheses on primordial space and time, all the points I scored that raised me to a level never before attained by an African . . . In a flash, I see all the Associates. I'm no longer anything but a vague memory in their eyes. Human existence! What is it? A bunch of good or bad memories. Every genius submits to this law. Immortality? A group of memories held in the minds of the living. Who am I now to them? For most of them, have our long discussions already dissolved in oblivion? And as for the flashes of insight that emanated from my genius, like fireflies lighting up the night sky of those Associates who adored me—I can hardly bring myself to believe that they have nothing but an ephemeral existence! I have relied on the Associates? A tactical error! They're gone. Among my so-called compatriots, I don't have a single friend. If I'd had even one, I wouldn't be subjected to this cruel law of silence. A silence of complicity, a silence of resignation! Even for Niaiseux, who at this very moment is expiating the fatality of History, I no longer represent anything. And the only person in the world with whom I could commune amid the opacity of consciences, is she in mourning? Is she staying in the seclusion that was our daily condition? My tender spouse! The cruel fate that has befallen me hounds her as well. The wall of incommunicability has grown thicker, more implacable. Here I am, like the being described by Robert Musil, "who cannot speak or be spoken of, who disappears silently among the mass of humanity, just a little scribble on the tablets of history, a creature like a snowflake falling in midsummer; am I real or a dream, good or evil, precious or worthless?"[80] My existence is useless. A dead weight. Dragged heavily down. I encounter nothing but hostility. What could I offer to barter for the smile that can't be refused to a human being? Nothing can light up my face. Solitude is my lover. I am denied even a look of scorn. Yet all these young men are the product of Western universities, just as much as I am! One thing brings us together: culture! They all hate me: hatred, a cultural trait! No, a fatality of nature dividing them and me. It is our sole common denominator. I have chosen; they have not. The choice is poles apart from nature. Their tales, their fables, their legends, their myths, their epics, that's what they call culture! All the same, constraints of nature. An intertwined bunch of determinisms, twisting the individual's neck to make him always look back at the past, to perpetuate the dialogue with the ancestors. Vanished from our universe, they remain present in a transparent form. Their speech escapes the reductive role that constitutes the screen of our culture. Has this seemingly free-floating speech had such weight that the passage of these young technocrats through the Western universities hasn't left any trace in them? Not even the possibility of choosing, which is the foundation of the act

---

80. From Musil's autobiographical novella "Tonka" (*"Tonka"* 184).

of culture? The Western dialectic liberates; the African one constrains, encloses, enslaves. At least to the extent that, who knows by what clever opening to the world, the presence of these young men becomes a way of taking Africa out of itself. That would really be a brilliant stroke of this bygone Africa, mistress of the symbolic! A hardly probable hypothesis for their leaders, crushed beneath the weight of the destiny of an entirely enslaving mode of thought. A miracle would have to have occurred here, to open them up to the need to submit themselves to the law of what some call the dialogue between cultures! In this hypothesis, that would be the technocrats' affirmative role.

As I unfold these thoughts, the trial procedure is being arranged. Great importance is evidently attached to this. In front of each head of delegation's chair is placed a stool, carved with the motifs suitable to each delegation's provenance. Even so, a common motif reappears from one stool to the next: the presence of a terrifying mask here, a menacing one there. The chairs themselves are decorated in the same fashion. But added to them are mysterious signs that seem to be a kind of writing particular to these sanctuaries, as it's very regular. Behind are placed the cultural technocrats.

A little time passes before the leaders enter. The technocrats come alive, exchanging ideas, busying themselves. Servants place garlands around masks that are hung in the four corners of the trial chamber. Every two yards, pylons hold skulls attached to their tops. In general, the decor remains very simple.

Placed in one corner of the scene, guarded by the gorilla who had worked on Niaiseux, I watch the servants going back and forth. The final touches are put on the decor. From moment to moment I wait to be put in the middle of the scene, like a sacrificial offering, or rather like the master of ceremonies. I'll be at the center of the debate, a debate whose absurdity makes clear in no uncertain manner that the accused has been condemned in advance. Of what, exactly, am I being accused? What is the competence of the judiciary that is sitting in judgment on me?

Hush! The counselors are all told to be quiet, for the chairmen are arriving to take their place at the tribunal. They enter according to the order established by African gerontocracy. They each have a fly whisk. Hats made entirely of multicolored pearls adorn their heads. Their clothing, made of fine raffia, consists essentially of a loincloth and a kind of tunic on which is embossed the escutcheon of the sanctuary of which each is the head.

After standing for a moment in reflection, the chairmen all sit down. A sign is made to my bodyguard to place me in the center of the scene. I go by myself, without waiting for the brute to offer me his services. A low murmur runs among those in attendance. No doubt, of indignation. A gesture by the hosting chairman suffices to reestablish silence. As is appropriate, his task is to set out for his peers the reasons for my arrest, after the eldest of them has opened the session.

Translation:

"Dear Comrades, you have all heard the echoes of recent events. You would not be here today if something serious had not occurred. Our organizational regulations forbid us to arrest anyone arbitrarily. If this fanatic is appearing before you, it is because we have determined that his crime passes all bounds.

"Some may find this trial unusual. Indeed, in the so-called free world, nothing of this sort exists. A trial based on an offense against culture! Inconceivable. Is it not the originality of our continent to have escaped the compartmentalizing of reality into political factors, economic factors, cultural factors, religious factors, and so on? Reality is more complex than that; every aspect is imbricated in the others. The sacred exists in the quotidian celebration of life. The rupture between the profane and the sacred is a crime for which the West feels remorse night and day—a Rousseauean remorse, to tell the truth, that leads a good number of intellectuals to seize on our rites, our myths, our sacrifices, in order to retrieve a lost innocence, a lost childhood. They look at childhood as the myth of the supposed

morning of the world. *They exercise themselves to find in this milieu a 'primordial chaos' of pure rhythm, pure duration, in which it seems that daybreak is not distinguished from nightfall. They assimilate us to this infancy, considered as the first stage of human evolution. Following this logic of the confusion of types and of contradictory elements, atheism is no longer opposed to unbelief, nor the profane to the sacred, nor hatred to love, nor contempt to esteem. This is the new and subtle form of exploitation forged by the West. If we do not watch out, the good God himself will let himself be caught, and one fine day we will find ourselves once again in the midst of subversion. It will be too late by the time we realize this. The secret of our vitality, of our creative power, lies in our rites and in our myths. Whoever appropriates the secret of a people's culture can make use of it at will. He can introduce destructive elements, can capture everything he wishes to promote. By now the West has reached the point of breaking open the secret mechanism of our myths; reduced to a system of operations, they are studied algebraically. We are no more than abstractions, manipulated by symbols from which our subjectivity has been completely emptied out. We still believe ourselves to possess a secret mythic discourse. Illusion. We no longer belong to ourselves. We are another's man. Anyone who doubts this need only recall how, having mastered the intimacy of matter, and having succeeded in subverting it through the bombardment of particles, the white man has shown at Hiroshima what he is capable of. He* has come to this point through an unheard-of audacity that defies everything; by a series of little thefts perpetuated by generation after generation across the millennia. It has not taken him even a century to pierce the mystery of our discourse. It has been stripped bare. Dissected, its fragments caught within concepts that form a mysterious algebra, understood only by a few initiates. Its laws of operation completely mastered. Not a single nook or cranny escapes them.

"Yet even so, there exists a domain in which we remain masters of our discourse, where we can take refuge without being disturbed. The full weight of our subjectivity is admirably incarnated by the storyteller: the untranscribable and untranslatable space-time continuum; the freedom of development, the dramatism of the gesture, of the word, of modulations, of calls, of requests, of interpellations, of the imaginary articulated by the body to the body of the dialogue, of the presence of the Other. An entire taboo realm. Forbidden, But of an infinite richness. Kaleidoscope of an infinity of languages. You can watch the storyteller imitate the language of the leopard, the lion, the hare, the fox, the old sorceress, the child. Doubling, redoubling, disguise, costuming, imitation, copy, and expressivity form this universe that today is to be dynamited, handed over to the foreigner. A criminal hand has been preparing to strike against us. But we have intervened just in time. It is now beyond harming us, for a long time to come. I have been speaking of this Dog of a stranger, whom you see here. Arisen from our earth—I dare not say from our race—he has nothing African about him but the skin that he would trade away at the first opportunity. By a coldly considered choice, he has scornfully turned his back on us. He has no belief in the dialogue of cultures. He is immured within an impregnable fortress: a haughty and aggressive solitude. We have followed him night and day. He has come to us on his own, in a movement of criminal provocation. Hear this, dear Comrades: seeking to establish a new écriture, instead of using the resources of his own 'culture' to give birth to his discourse, he has turned to Africa. Oh! Sacrilege! Our rites of initiation and of magic! This atheist has dared to attain the sacred, he who professes himself an unbeliever. Our culture only interests him to serve his ambition. Traitor! This is a new kiss of Judas.[81]

"And more. Through his gestural écriture, he wishes to deliver our last refuge to the enemy. It is ourselves, it is our children, it is our wives whom he betrays. A slaver's supreme gesture. Having sold our secret, he can do with us what he will. Our intimacy violated and desacralized, we will be made into prostitutes. Who among us could remain indifferent in the face of such crimes?

"We have always cultivated friendship among peoples. The gesture of this Dog was leading to the germs of war being

---

81. The speaker evokes the kiss of betrayal by which Judas identifies Jesus to the crowd that comes to seize him in the Garden of Gethsemane (Matt. 26.47–50).

planted both in the West—his new fatherland—and among us in Africa. Among us, he exposed our nudity, our space, in order to deliver them like slaves to the West's written discourse. For them, the receivers, both the themes and the imaginary of our people were equally paving the way toward enslavement. Judas of Modernity, are you aware of the enormity of your crime?

"Worse yet. In the West, so as to be authentic, artistic experience proceeds through what they term the systematic derangement of all the senses[82]—the experience of an unfathomable abyss, of the utterly other. Coming to us, you have assimilated our rites to these sessions of sensual derangement! How could you have dared to place our rites in parallel with all the vices to which the Western artists give themselves over? Drugs, marijuana, hashish, alcohol, unnatural vices? It was entirely your right to make yourself vicious, maudit, autoerotic, but—and here is the rub—you exceeded the limits of this right when, with perverse intentions, you denatured our sacrificial ceremonies, despite the premonitions of our ancestors.

"Even in the West these miraculous weapons were going to be received as shots launched by black cannons. We would have been taken for irresponsible! Who would take responsibility for such a war? Our weapons would have caused their writing

---

82. Echoing the French poet Rimbaud, who declared in 1871 that "le Poète se fait voyant par un long, immense et raisonné dérèglement de tous les sens" ("the poet makes himself into a seer by a long, immense, and reasoned derangement of all the senses"; Œuvres 251).

to disintegrate, becoming an echo chamber for every ideological revolution, a concentration-camp hell in which the ebb and flow of thought continually despoils every ideology of its dogmatic aura, perpetually accused by every anterior writing.

"You will agree with me, dear Comrades, that it was not for us to deliver our secrets to this foreign Dog in order to poison in the West what constitutes a latent tendency to subversion. We cultivate friendship as our ancestors have always done. African philosophy forbids us to give ourselves over to provocation. This is why I consider this Stranger as someone irresponsible. He thus should suffer an exemplary punishment; I have spoken."

During this long indictment, which has concluded in the best prosecutorial traditions, I listen attentively and observe the advisors' reactions. They are fully in approval. A few minutes' break. The chieftains and the counselors consult and come to agreement. The eloquence of the host chieftain and of his aide is persuasive.

The session resumes. The floor is immediately given to another counselor.

"Comrade, you have spoken well. Africa has been insulted. This boundless offense requires reparations. All the same, we cannot ignore the repercussions that this unprecedented trial will have, notably how it is assessed in the world and in Africa itself. This treasonous crime—this sacrilege, this atheistic attempt to appropriate and hand over to the enemy our most intimate secrets and our most sacred patrimony—must be suppressed. It is Africa's duty and inalienable right to defend her cultural patrimony. Africa has long been pillaged. Just look at the British Museum! What a scandal! Systematic pillaging of ancient Egypt. The Louvre! The Tervuren![83] The vandalism that characterized the first contacts of the West with Africa should not be repeated. The emptying of Africa's riches will always constitute one of the crimes that weighs upon Europe's conscience. We still allow them to siphon off our primary materials, our works of art. But when they go as far as to touch our subjectivity, so as to force us to move from the realm of subjectivity to be objectified, this is what angers us! We declare: Halt, rascals! Having reduced us to slavery, having depersonalized us, not content with the domination installed in the very heart of our continent, now they do violence to our discourse. They want to submit our tales' linear and orderly development to their own narrative protocols. The violence of 'logical sequences,' a teleological violence glibly exercised by unscrupulous semanticists! The violence of a savage vivisection of our tales. The violence of a brutal symbolization in which our realities are entirely dehumanized. Are we forever to silently sit by in the face of this sort of vandalism? Of this demoralizing, exploitative, debilitating, emasculating ethnocentrism?

---

83. Belgium's Royal Museum for Central Africa, established in 1897 to showcase King Leopold's possessions and to advertise the king's "civilizing mission" in the Congo.

"Our discourse, brutally inserted into theirs, no longer shows an awareness of anything in particular but is regarded as an awareness of pure relations. We would willingly have allowed their subjectivity to adopt our words. But unceremoniously and carelessly torn away from our own words, we become objectified in a game of conceptual relations. With our words' sociocultural articulation emptied out, and with it the accumulated experience of generations, it is the path to enslavement that we perpetuate, a rope around our neck. Do we shrug our shoulders? No, Comrades, let us act!"

A third advisor:

"Comrades, the West, together with all its spiritual offspring, are at a crossroads. They are looking for ways to alter culture. I ask myself: Why is the price to be paid for this the subjugation of the Other? The effort of this Dog could have been an interesting case of cultural dialogue. But with the problem badly posed at the outset, we have been launched on a dead-end path. Whatever may be the verdict of this trial, the Assembly has to keep the world from believing that Africa refuses all dialogue. Our trial has less to do with the question of knowing whether Western discourse can nourish itself with African discourse than with the processes of our discourse's enslavement and violation. The question of dialogue, of symbiosis between discourses arising from heterogeneous cultures, has to be posed on the level of principles. These are what escape us. We have no *grasp of them at all. In this order of ideas, this alienated man, brought before us today, continues to enjoy his most sacred rights. He is free to posit that the imaginary discourse—the novel—that haunts his dreams could exist in a mode of osmosis with the African imaginary—the tale. His credo leads him to believe that the novel could develop itself by espousing the pathways of our tales. Naivete? Audacity? No matter. We have to settle upon what we believe to be a crime."*

Assorted movements can be seen among the counselors. Some approving, others disapproving. Several of them ask to speak. The debate seems to center on the processes that led me to the attempt to appropriate their discourse. They don't seem interested in the principle of osmosis between discourses. They don't want to risk going down a road whose end is uncertain. In effect, it seems a challenging task to enclose within one discourse a discourse taken from a different culture whose lifeblood consists of specific themes, symbols, myths. It would be necessary to demonstrate the theoretical possibility of doing so, to set it on solid grounds. Establish its absorption in the new structure and its fertilizing effects. Cultures—fabrics of images, of structuring symbols, of systems of representation. Could one demonstrate scientifically the possibility of subterranean flows of communication? Through watertight, impermeable subsoil?

Through communicating vessels?[84] What artist could hope to drill down to such subterranean depths? To open connections between heterogeneous but equally invigorating water tables? An illusion? True artists dig down to this layer. Those who cannot do so resemble desiccated mandrakes, lacking their fertilizing silt. When its roots are forked, a tree grips only surface sediments, deceptively covering over fructifying formations.

Imaginative discourse sinks its roots into the discourse of social life, projected into men's fantasies, dreams, desires; into possible worlds. *Écriture* is the evocation of these fictions. To suppose that it can drink deep in the social discourse of another people, to tame it in the way that "one encloses the Other within structure," would seem to be a crime of presumption. This is why artists don't dare to venture into such slippery terrain.

Impatient, another counselor speaks up.

"Comrades, we have heard your discussion. Several of you have said very lovely things. I would like to ask a fundamental question. Do we have the right to conduct this trial? Upon what basis can we arrest an individual and judge him under the heading of atheism? The solidity of the debate rests upon this basis. An alienated son of the country claims to have cut

---

84. In *Les vases communicants* (1932), André Breton argued that society could be revolutionized by uniting into an organic whole the "communicating vessels" of everyday reality and the world of dreams.

the umbilical cord that connected him to his mother Africa. He is most certainly a renegade! Monstrous! But does this authorize us to judge him? Can someone tell me this?"

A West African counselor:

"Do you suppose that we would have come here without a serious and substantial reason? That the trial we have begun would then be arbitrary? Would you have sold us out and been alienated from us? Comrades, it is time to close ranks. We are starting to stray. It may be desirable to recall certain elementary principles of the rights of peoples and of nations. Every people has the right to internal and external security. All measures that lead to the assurance of this double security are not just morally permissible but are obligatory. No nation can take them away. These can be preventive measures, as it is better to prevent war than to wage it. The law of peoples and of nations recognizes this.

"As far as our trial is concerned, has our security been threatened? Externally as well as internally? If the response to these questions is in the affirmative, we have the solid juridical basis that we seek. I defy anyone to contradict me."

A counselor from Central Africa:

"The questions as formulated by our West African comrade seem to me pertinent and sufficiently circumscribed to give our debate an unassailable juridical basis. Has our security been threatened? Yes! Has it in fact been attacked as much from outside as from within? Yes!"

A massive yes greets these proposals here and there among the Assembly. The last orator seems to have helped the young university graduates who were becoming bogged down in meanderings and in a spiral like the zigzags drawn by children. Is the trial approaching its conclusion?

"*I ask that the verdict be rendered without delay. All those who seek the security of a state know what they are waiting for: that a just punishment be inflicted upon this fanatic.*"

The youngest of the counselors breaks out in indignation:

"*Comrades, I have heard all the orators with interest.*"

"*Nothing more is needed!*" a thunderous voice from the Assembly replies.

"*I have been struck,*" the young counselor continues, "*by the justice of the various proposals. Each orator has made his contribution to clarifying this debate, which could have fallen into the worst of confusions. But the African genius, that of our ancestors—alas!—watches over us, and it has saved us from universal scorn. All the same, I ask myself if this is truly the time to pronounce such a verdict. Have we exhausted the subject, returned seven times to the arguments, or as the Warega say,[85] did we 'take two steps, three steps'? Any hastiness would be prejudicial to the criminal's cause and equally to ours. I am*

---

85. The Warega are a Congolese ethnic group.

always horrified by terrorism, whether it arises from any kind of intolerance or from the most down-to-earth fascism. It is most dangerous when it is intellectual. Africa's health does not lie in abdicating its own self for the sake of conformism. In undertaking this trial, our intention has not been to construct a Great Wall of China around our continent, to prevent our intellectuals from engaging in dialogue with colleagues elsewhere. The greatest malady that Africa suffers today is the new ideology—found almost everywhere—that seeks a pronounced unanimity. Idem velle, idem nolle.[86] Pluralism has become a crime. I ask myself this question: progress, or regression? From the remotest times, our continent, wrapped up in a collective narcissism through the constraints and fatalities of history, has kept us going only through idle chatter, in which we are content with a specular image of ourselves. Our discourse has never managed to liberate itself from the constraints of mythic thinking, the highest stage of unanimism. We have always been raised on this: unanimity around a dogmatic system in which a critical spirit and pluralism of opinions have been nonexistent. Is not our attitude today toward this young man that of a woman jealous over her lover? Her treasure that she doesn't let anyone see, for fear that others will steal it?

"Let me make myself clear. Far be it from me to approve everything this young man has done. But I would like to draw

---

86. "Same desires, same dislikes," an old Roman adage.

our attention to a widespread ideology, the Africanist ideology, that wants African realities to be unique, original. What one of our comrades has just called 'an assault on our security' is nothing more than 'an assault on our specificity,' on our withdrawal within ourselves. But let us not forget that a 'specificity' prepares its own asphyxiation insofar as it receives no oxygen from outside. Cultures survive only by opening up to other cultures that can liberate them from their tendency to collective narcissism. Is the initiative of the accused really so culpable? Would it not be better to see in it the boldness of a young researcher who has tried to liberate our discourse from its infirmities, opening it up to a more theoretical and universal discourse? If he had succeeded as an author, would he not have founded a revolutionary theory of the novel? What enrichment, for us and for the West! For humanity! A new science of écriture, whose founder would have been a Black? Who would have remained unmoved? The West has had its Marx, its Freud; Africa has not yet had one. Will we eternally keep on following others? The only thing we've been able to display to the world has been rhythmic percussion, elevated today by some African nations to the level of Black uniqueness. All day long, the dazed masses give themselves over to sessions of debauchery, rediscovering the primitive rhythmicity that colonization has put on the back burner. Yet the problem raised by this trial is important. Either we devote ourselves to Africa's regression or else we open ourselves to progress."

This penetrating speech doesn't seem to be very moving. The majority of faces don't hide their disapproval.

"My brilliant, university-trained Comrade, your speech is seductive. But you back away from the problem. For in the end, it is precisely a question of deciding whether the opening of African discourse to a more theoretical and universal model constitutes an attack on the continent's internal and external security and thus deserves an exemplary punishment. Has there been aggression, or at least an attempt at aggression? Everything hangs upon that. Let us not ramble on any further. Let us keep the arguments sharply focused."

This last intervention only seems to increase the confusion of the debate. Tempers begin to get heated. Those who'd thought the problem resolved along one line no longer seem as positive as they'd been at the start. Although the discussion has attained a high level, it has reached an impasse. All of the young counselors try to speak up, more from the wish to show off what they've learned in their different Western universities than from any concern to help the trial move along. With each intervention, things seem to be sinking further into byzantinism. How to untangle things? The trial is no longer about Giambatista but is a confrontation of the counselor-assistants; the only good thing about their oratorial jousting is that it hasn't degenerated into outright brawling.

As for the heads of delegation, they don't seem to understand anything at all of their juniors' discussions. They had been assembled to pronounce judgment on a traitor, a blasphemer, an atheist who, driven by criminal audacity, had raised his hand against their most sacred rites. That is what was to be judged. Many of them are growing impatient with the counselors' often pedantic and exhibitionistic quibbles.

With an imperious gesture, the oldest of the chairmen obtains silence.

"Was the traitor given the truth potion," he asks, "at the start of the trial?"

"No," replies a chorus of the host sanctuary.

"How could you have neglected such an essential rite in a trial? You young people are showing off, but no one thinks to interrogate the accused?"

At that very instant, everyone turns toward me. I read in the eyes of the chairmen something like a sense of satisfaction caused by the inability of the young intellectuals to conduct a gathering. Throughout the oratorical jousting, the chairmen said nothing; they looked on; they sneered beneath their beards.

"Bring me a goat, and the vessel for potions."

The animal is brought forward. It is decapitated with a single sword stroke, and two men hold it over the vessel to collect its blood. An impressive silence falls among the Assembly.

The mixture of blood with the liquid that has just been brought constitutes the sanctuaries' most solemn potion. It is only resorted to in exceptional circumstances. In my case, the matter is clear: the prosecutor allows no doubt as to the gravity of the case.

A shiver passes through me from head to toe. And at that moment, a verse from Michel Leiris arises from the depths of my heart: "The octopus distends its arms of blood; / Five tentacles, five arms of steel . . ."[87] Image of primitive humanity that dies in a universe of death and destruction; of terror and shock; of the eroticization of blood, fear, and horror.

The sacrificed goat is supposed to lend assistance through a magical relation with the person to be sacrificed, in hopes of a release of truth and a successful result. Giambatista is being killed in me, so that the Black can be reborn. The mixing of the goat's blood with my own in this masochistic and sadistic rite will render more

---

87. From the surrealist poet and ethnographer Michel Leiris's "Le chasseur de têtes" ("The Headhunter"; *Haut mal* 44; 43–45), in which an African headhunter sees octopi as floating severed heads.

authentic the rapport between the audience and me. At least they will believe him. A proof, and a test. Fettering forever the possibility of my success in the novelistic art. The death of Western discourse—of that gestural transcription of my direct interior experience that I have desired, inspired by orality, married in a dynamic union with writing. Africa was right after all! And yet without any truth!

They have me sit in the middle on a stool. The potion does its work. My legs, heavy and as if magnetized, hold me fast. My hands are tied behind my back. Yet no physical violence is done to me. The rain of injuries that they have customarily unleashed on their victim seems to have ceased. That's because they are now sure that I am in their power. From the point of view of everyone looking at me, in this public and exposed arena, I am like the Christian victims whom the Romans handed over to the lions. What sadistic pleasure are they seeking? Does the pursuit of their truth require going "as far as blood, knowing that castigation is good for firming up the flesh"?[88] Isn't it too easy to pick off an unseduced victim? Beaten down, like a prostitute who offers herself, what further theme of conquest can I offer them?

---

88. A quotation from Leiris's hallucinatory novel *Aurora* (87), from a scene in which a temple priest abuses his female slaves.

With my discourse slain, speech is instantly reborn in me and restores me to their universe: universe of the immediate, of the hesitant, of the fleeting, of spontaneous associations, universe of no return. I've exchanged the Gutenberg Galaxy for an imaginary flight from the world.[89] I am plunged into a river without riverbanks where I am forbidden to bathe twice. I've recovered the jubilant mimicry that speech offers the primitive in his self-presence. Abandoning of the self, refusal of conquest, resignation of the self.

Why this obstinate refusal to offer myself as a victim? This pigheadedness? What instinct remains for me to assuage? I don't have a breath left to draw. I have had my springtime and my summer. Summer has fled at the arrival of autumn. Conquered, my leaves fallen, stripped of the luminous dress of summer, I am nothing more than a prematurely extinguished star.

With what can I oppose them? My weakness? Absurd! With indifference? Stranger to them that I am! At this point, my defeat is their victory. The only seed of hope is to bring me back to them. An end that strangely echoes my career, which resonated at the outset with the cry of failure.

---

89. In *The Gutenberg Galaxy* (1962), Marshall McLuhan analyzed the impact of the mass media on "typographic man."

"Young man," the chairman addresses me, "one of our proverbs says: 'Only foreigners eat the bitter fern.' And another: 'He who finds himself in the grip of a hawk doesn't get sunburned, only the one who's carried on its back.' I do not know your theories on the judicial art. But we have a wisdom, handed down from generation to generation, that is equal if not superior to what the Whites have taught you. Thanks to it, our societies enjoy an internal equilibrium. We have nothing to regret or to search for elsewhere in this particular domain. Yet know that an animal never forgets his tracks. You have tried to make us believe that you were not one of us. You have bothered us day and night, professing to be a renegade. You did not do this blindly. You knowingly seized onto our rites. You knew what awaited you. Severe, sibylline premonitions should have indicated this to you. A proverb teaches us: 'If there are no fish in the pond, don't let your children be killed by the mosquitos there.' That is why 'a tortoise who falls into a hole can debate all she likes; she isn't going to get out.' Listen carefully: are you deserving of pardon?"

"..."

"You do not reply! One of your proverbs says: 'Forewarned is forearmed.' When you made contact with us in order to become a great writer, were you unaware of the risk you were running? You know well that 'if you

142

befriend a bee, get yourself a good supply of palm trees, for bees love palm wine!'"

"..."

"You do not reply! We were dead to you. Why did you return to trouble our sleep? Did you not know that 'you never use stolen money to bury a corpse'? And 'bury a debtor early in the day to avoid his creditors'?"

"..."

"You do not reply![90] Because I speak to you in proverbs! And yet they are the mother's milk that nourished you, that furnished your mind! 'Remembering is a sign of wisdom; forgetting a sign of idiocy.' 'When you go too fast, you miss the turn.' This is your case. You are in our hands today, and we will not just let you leave. You are condemned to perform the Return to the Native Land.[91] Will you pass the remainder of your days among us? You will come to know, one by one, the joys of living in one place today, another the next. Until you have made the rounds of our villages eighty-seven times eighty-seven times."

Sustained applause. Everyone cries out, "Wisdom has spoken!" "He couldn't say a single word against the

---

90. At his trial before Pontius Pilate, Jesus refused three times to answer charges against him (Matt. 27).

91. Citing Césaire's 1939 *Cahier d'un retour au pays natal* (*Notebook of a Return to the Native Land*), in which the poet envisioned a hallucinatory return from Paris to his homeland of Martinique.

indictment." "African wisdom has taken him away from the alleged Western rhetoric that he was spouting." "If he who abandoned our culture to embrace a supposedly more authentic one is unable to come up with a single word in his native tongue, how could he possibly manage to plumb the depths of the language of the Whites, who don't even bathe in the same water as we do?" "He's a charlatan." "That's all he deserves to be called." "That's right, that's well said." "His imposture has been unmasked."

"If you try to climb hills," the chairman continues, "you will sleep in the brush; if you set yourself to admire lovely women, your eyes will ache. You are the lark that has found a winged ant, but they go to those who have bigger bellies. And thus, you should take yourself to the school of wisdom. You are like the Israelite who makes his way back to Zion after two thousand years of wandering. The palm wine of the desert is far too rich to welcome the prodigal son."

Thunderous applause. Hysterical cries issue from every mouth. The crowd is delirious. Joyful chidbirth. Eternal Africa! The group seems to be welded together in its communion, more by words than through real action. This is why a number of African nations are driven into deliriums of verbal metamorphoses pompously baptized "revolutions." Words! Their magical sack full of game.

"Speech comes from men just as feathers come from birds. Silence is the prison of speech. It can free itself if it takes refuge in sighs."

"That's striking!" "That's hit the nail on the head!" "A writing lesson like we've never seen!" "Such a lesson has never been given in the memory of man!" "The cassava that you grill on an empty stomach revives your energy right away!"

The chairman is continually interrupted by noisy cheers. Everything he says is punctuated by frenetic applause. It gives the impression that he is literally liberating his world from an eschatological misfortune and a collective suppression.

I haven't proffered a single word since the trial began. My silence is interpreted as defeat. Or better: as disalienation, as a conversion. Silence is golden, speech too rich in hope, treacherous.

So I am a man condemned. Rejected. Torn away from one society and hurled into another! What fate is this? Reintegration or eternal banishment? Isn't every condemnation a rejection by human society? They meant to get me back, but haven't they lost me for good? I've escaped from a dungeon only to occupy a larger one with the dimensions of Africa. I have heard my sentence

145

without showing the least feeling. No one is looking at me. The delirium inspired by the chairman's words removes me from their world for as long as they keep laughing. Once the euphoria has passed, their stares will plunge me back into the dungeon. I've forbidden myself to show anything, not even a nod of my head. To let any feeling at all be visible would have been taken as a sign of hope. I've refused to be complicit with myself. Revolt, indifference are the seeds of hope. But I have been condemned from the moment of my arrest. Not a ray of sunlight can be seen on my horizon. "My people" have torn me from "my world" in order to throw me into the prison of eternity. My crime is to have been cut off from their communion. Their entire judicial apparatus was nothing but the staging of a mirror in which I could read my condition; our condition. Narcissistic gaze. Specular image. A bitterly jubilatory mix of irony and tension. A crime? Isn't it that of all humanity? Of the avoided look. Of the narrowed eyes. Of unrealized desire. Of suppression. Of art. Of creation's unpredictability. Of *écriture*: mélange of thoughts, dreams, fantasies, expectations, thrown together in a "sum of meditation and expression," according to *le mot juste* of Bachelard.[92]

---

92. Citing Gaston Bachelard's definition of "l'homme littéraire" ("the literary man") in the writer's 1943 essay on the imagination, *L'air et les songes* (*Air and Dreams*; 302).

Masters of dramatization, they have slaked their thirst for crime and have almost reached their desired goal. I was the designated victim. They had thought to see me fall into the trap of revolt and of asking for pity. They didn't deserve that easy treat. That would have meant giving them a chance to recognize themselves in me, to recognize a brother. The executioner has no right to any light of dawn. He cuts himself off from any reconciling look. Human justice—an implacable, crapulous machine. A *danse macabre*. Indefensible orgy. Epitome of human history. And are they actors? As a matter of fact, spectators. I offered them the power to read their own condition. The abyss that separated me from them is the very same as the one that renders each of them a stranger to the others in the Assembly. Far from uniting them, my spectacle has made them more distant than ever, from each other and from the rest of humankind. The proverbial solidarity of Africa is only an opium of disunity. But didn't my condemnation seal the pact of opacity that adhered to the human condition?

Condemned to wandering—me, GIAMBATISTA! Why did they even bother to mitigate their criminal plan? Wouldn't an outright execution have been better? To go from one cultural area to the next—that's to say, from oblivion to oblivion! I will no sooner have left one area for another than the horizon of oblivion will have swallowed me up. In the medieval and immemorial darkness of Africa. In that halo of the Dark Continent that dissolves personalities into anonymity. Return to that gloomy time of primitive space. Here I am, marginalized! Enveloped in a kind of polluting fog. All those who have condemned me—polluters! Didn't the speech of the old chieftain that triggered the delirium resemble the smog that pollutes our cities? Garbage, trash! To think that they feasted on my spectacle as on a bottle of Antillean rum! How to bring Africa out of the thick fog of savagery? Curled up on herself like a piece of paper in the heat, today she is guided by a few myths that leave us dreaming! Her peoples, only barely awakened, allow themselves to be led like lambs to the slaughter on the altars of the gods. Immolated on the altars of Revolution, of Democracy, realities that are nonetheless ungraspable under the sky of the feudal monarchs who swarm across the continent! Verbal inflation, delirium of words, new sauce called for to season African politics. The haggard masses plunged into collective hallucinations in broad daylight. Socialism, African Path, and revolution constitute the scaffolds on which they are sacrificed; underdevelopment, their guillotine. Themselves condemned by an implacable mechanism! Punished by the god Capital. Marginalization! Periphery! Cruel euphemisms! The truth: unequal exchange, new form of tragedy. The gods, vanquished by human foolishness, have been killed. The masses are taken to the slaughterhouse without ever having been convicted. A handful of executioners assassinate them daily, little by little. *Stop!* Stop it, you bunch of wretched criminals! You have a name: the privileged! How long will we have to bear the constraints of your mythology? ENOUGH OF THIS OUTRAGE![93]

This last cry, which I had thought purely obsessive had, in fact, overflowed my internal discourse. I woke up from my fantasies with a start. Instinctively I rubbed my eyes, readjusted my glasses, took a deep breath. I looked around. I was alone. Alone. The Assembly had dispersed, and I hadn't noticed. Alone on center stage! Since when? Were they going to return and continue the trial? Was their departure a kind of return to deliberation? Perhaps for a week? Had my condemnation not yet taken effect, then? No, that's a Western way of looking at things!

They want to register their specificity. The African way deserves its place in the sun. As an aside? Generally that doesn't last long, and that's on the stage! Would they trust a condemned man enough to leave me alone in the open air? I try to take some steps. To my great surprise,

---

93. This phrase, "ASSEZ DE CE SCANDALE!" in the French, is a quotation from Césaire's *Cahier d'un retour au pays natal* (32), in which Césaire protested against the exploitation of the Caribbean, including native women, by white colonists.

it's as though I'm nailed to the ground; as if iron bands are keeping me in place. No doubt, I tell myself, it's the effect of the truth potion. That's what explains the confidence they have in leaving me alone.

All at once cries and the beating of tom-toms resound in the distance, combined with modern music. I understand! They're celebrating! They're celebrating their victory and the heads of the delegations. They've thrown themselves into it without giving their victim another thought. Such parties generally last several days. Amid the general inebriation, will they still remember me? I was already facing the walls of ostracism even before the delegations had quitted the sanctuary of the trial! I've been consigned to "the Gulag Archipelago" of oblivion.[94] The waters of Lethe are leading me to infinitely distant shores, to a nameless gulf. I see an immense host of innocent people being thrown in, carried by the furious waves to be devoured by sea monsters. The gods, divorced from mankind, mindlessly assist in the spectacle. "They laughed among themselves, they joked, they sneered." Their sardonic laughter led to deadly sneezing. Our eyes were blindfolded, the peepers. What—out of

---

94. Referring to *The Gulag Archipelago* (1973), Aleksandr Solzhenitsyn's history of the network of Soviet forced labor camps where many dissidents were imprisoned.

pity? That's long gone, replaced by the "yellow pass-port."[95] Overflow of satiated murderous hatreds. Rise and fall of the tide of the living dead. In the blink of an eye, millions and millions of men are taken on this voyage toward the oblivion of insects. No solidarity can overcome it. Fatality of which we are the daily artisans. Every day hunted down, suppressed, loaded onboard and deported, confined by malevolent desires that receive some kind of bonus of pleasure from doing so. How to stop these successive waves that oblivion drags behind it in the Gulag Archipelago? Humans always finish the race in the same way. The seed of oblivion is encrusted in their flesh. It gnaws away, day and night, like a cancer. The human tide, condemned to this destiny, has no other outlet than this unequal combat against the monsters of the void. Niaiseux, already swallowed up in the abyss, must be stretching out his hand to me! At this moment I may be the only one who can bring him back into existence! He lives again. Are human beings unable to overcome this discontinuity that makes them oscillate between nothingness and existence? Each of us is Lazarus, Christ.[96]

---

95. An identity card that former convicts had to carry in nineteenth-century France.
96. Both the dead man brought back to life and his savior (John 11).

I'd briefly lost track of the music and the beating of the tom-toms. My eyes were open, but I couldn't see anything around me. I was embarked on an interior journey. Entrenched within myself, I contemplated monsters, air bubbles, fireflies, shooting stars. Lurking within my dreams, I was forgetting the human world. They have prevented me from writing the book that would have constituted the Copernican revolution of the novel. But the interior monologue that I've been writing ever since my arrest is beyond their grasp and their power, free from all the apparatus of fettered gestures, on the threshold of the dawning of expression; they are unable to submit that to the constraint of censorship. Drawn from our background, my interior discourse freely elaborates itself, established in its own reality, sheltered from the public, powerful enough to allow me to extract from my intimate moments and my fantasies the image of my public, that internal parent indispensable for our artistic survival. Writing, you are a traitress! You enfold yourself in the prostitution of the body. Sadistic union. You approach speech as an easy prey. She gives herself over, like a streetwalker. You hunt speech down the way a man pursues a woman he covets, seizes, and penetrates. Prostitute, you give yourself to every ideology. From the dawn of humanity, those of the dominant class have come to flirt with you. You bore them a child: slavery. You've always been on the side of the dirty bourgeois.

The dancing has redoubled in intensity and has pierced my deafness. Still not a soul around me. Perhaps I was being surveilled by an invisible eye. One that peered at me, undressed me, and dressed me up again according to the tom-tom's rhythm. But I didn't try to find out. The thick silence enveloping me betrayed that of my interior solitude, however peopled by creatures evoked by my interminable waking dreams.

Suddenly I saw a human form appear before me. Phantom! "A man!" I exclaimed to myself. It had been an eternity since I'd seen anyone. Looking like an old market woman. Tousled hair. Tangled beard. I rubbed my eyes. The man approached. But he seemed to be impeded in his approach, concealing something between his legs. Having come a few paces from my throne, he stopped in order to peer at me. He smiled at me then deliberately advanced slowly toward me. I heard the sound of his bell. I recognized Niaiseux.

"Niaiseux!"

"Giambatista Viko!"

He threw himself at my knees. But I remained immobilized.

"Giambatista! Fate. Fatality. Destiny! Now you are Giambatista Viko. You are no longer *le Maître!*"

"What have you been doing since we were separated?"

"Wandering around the grounds, the vast grounds of the sanctuary. This is my condition. Humanity has become a stranger to me. The companionship of animals makes more sense than that of people. This is what wandering is! Far from people. The ringing that you've just heard serves to alert women. That is the sole communion I have with them. With men, scorn, hatred. I am a pariah. Brother animals—dogs, cats—they are legion on this property—caress me; I caress them. We understand each other. No one is paying any attention to them. Or to me. We live as companions wandering in nature. We hate hope."

"Indeed! Hoping kills when every horizon is blocked."

"We are guinea pigs."

"Guinea pigs for the death of hope! Knights errant in the Middle Ages went in quest of adventures, of 'spiritual matters.' But as for us, we are Galahads without a Grail. The men who could have set out on the most miraculous quest are dead. Our adventure is no more than the novel of the sacrament of nothingness."

"It seems that way, at least! But couldn't our novel be a sacrament of initiation to this return to nature, to clear air, to birdsong, to evening breezes caressing the leaves, bending the green grass! Ah, this return to nature that Western culture so eagerly seeks! Would that be a kind of lesson? Reconciling us with the organic, with the body, with nature; reintegrating us in the universe from which we've been separated by reason and culture!"

"But for this nature to be somehow reborn in us, is it necessary to kill the human?"

"Yes, resuscitate the bestial so that the human can rediscover himself, can recover his true form!"

"Which resides in the equilibrium of reason and nature."

"The price of this renaissance is the funeral of reason!"

After this brief dialogue, I could tell that Niaiseux had stayed himself despite this immersion in nature. His lucidity remained flawless. Instead of brutalizing him, the baptism by fire had restored him to himself. Without dialogue with the Other, we end up with a sense of regression. Mere illusion! But what is life but a sum of illusions!

Works Cited in the Novel and in Notes

Althusser, Louis. "Idéologie et appareils idéologiques d'état (notes pour une recherche)." *Positions (1964–1975)*, Les Éditions Sociales, 1976, pp. 67–125.

———. "Ideology and Ideological State Apparatuses (Notes toward an Investigation)." *"Lenin and Philosophy" and Other Essays*, translated by Ben Brewster, Verso, 1970, pp. 127–88.

Amrouche, Jean. *Journal, 1928–1962*. Éditions Alpha, 2009.

Arsan, Emmanuelle. *Emmanuelle*. Éditions Fixot, 1988.

Bachelard, Gaston. *L'air et les songes: Essai sur l'imagination et du mouvement*. José Corti, 1943.

Bécaud, Gilbert. Lyrics to "Quand il est mort, le poète." *Genius*, 2021, genius.com/Gilbert-becaud-quand-il-est-mort-le-poete-lyrics.

Breton, André. *Second Manifesto of Surrealism*. 1930. *Manifestoes of Surrealism*, by Breton, translated by Richard Seaver and Helen R. Lane, U of Michigan P, 1969, pp. 117–94.

Buffon, Comte de. *Discours sur le style*. Edited by Félix Hémon, 5th ed., Charles Delagrave, 1894. epub.ub.uni-muenchen.de/41202/1/8P.gall.2269.pdf.

Césaire, Aimé. *Cahier d'un retour au pays natal*. Présence Africaine, 1983.

———. *The Complete Poetry of Aimé Césaire: Bilingual Edition*. Translated by A. James Arnold and Clayton Eshleman, Wesleyan UP, 2017.

Desnos, Robert. *Corps et biens*. 1930. Bibliothèque Numérique Romande, 2016. ebooks-bnr.com/ebooks/pdf4/desnos_corps_et_biens.pdf.

Fabian, Johannes. *Time and the Other*. Columbia UP, 2014.

Goethe, Johann Wolfgang von. *Faust*. Translated by Victor Lange, Continuum, 1994.

Hugo, Adèle. *Victor Hugo raconté par Adèle Hugo*. Edited by Evelyn Blewer et al., Plon, 1985.

Lacan, Jacques. *Écrits*. Éditions du Seuil 1966.

Leiris, Michel. *Aurora*. Éditions Gallimard, 1946.

———. *Haut mal*. Éditions Gallimard, 1943.

Lévy-Bruhl, Lucien. *Les carnets*. PU de France, 1998.

Malraux, André. *Les noyers de l'Altenburg*. Éditions Gallimard, 1948.

———. *The Walnut Trees of Altenburg.* Translated by A. W. Fielding, Howard Fertig, 1989.

Marx, Karl. Introduction. *A Contribution to the Critique of Hegel's Philosophy of the Right.* 1844. *Marxist Internet Archive,* 2009, www.marxists.org/archive/marx/works/1843/critique-hpr/intro.htm.

Meadows, Donella H., et al. *The Limits to Growth.* Universe Books, 1972.

Michelet, Jules. *Histoire de France.* Edited by Claude Mettra, Éditions Rencontre, 1965.

Musil, Robert. *"Tonka" and Other Stories.* Translated by Eithne Wilkins and Ernst Kaiser, Secker and Warburg, 1965.

Ngal, Georges. "Introduction à une lecture d'*Epitomé* de Tchicaya U Tam'si." *Canadian Journal of African Studies,* vol. 9, no. 3, 1975, pp. 523–30.

———. "Le théâtre d'Aimé Césaire: Une dramaturgie de la décolonisation." *Revue des sciences humaines,* vol. 35, 1970, pp. 613–36.

Proust, Marcel. *À l'ombre des jeunes filles en fleurs.* Du côté de chez Swann, À l'ombre des jeunes filles en fleurs, pp. 431–955. *À la recherche du temps perdu,* edited by Pierre Clarac and André Ferré, vol. 1, Éditions Gallimard, 1954.

———. *Within a Budding Grove. In Search of Lost Time,* translated by C. K. Scott Moncrieff and Terence Kilmartin, revised by D. J. Enright, vol. 2, Random House, 1992.

Revel, Jean-François. *Ni Marx ni Jésus: La nouvelle revolution mondiale est commencée aux États-Unis.* 1970. Rev. ed., J'ai Lu, 1973.

Rimbaud, Arthur. *Œuvres complètes.* Edited by Antoine Adam, Éditions Gallimard, 1972.

Rowell, Margit. *La peinture, le geste, l'action: L'existentialisme en peinture.* Klincksieck, 1972.

Senghor, Léopold Sédar. "Le français, langue de culture." *Esprit,* Nov. 1962, pp. 837–44.

Vigny, Alfred de. *Œuvres complètes.* Edited by Paul Viallaneix, Éditions du Seuil, 1965.